THE CHASM

NIDHI LEKHARAJU

INDIA • SINGAPORE • MALAYSIA

ISBN 979-8-89556-383-0

To my beloved parents,

Who believed in me even when I didn't.

Contents

Prologue

The Portal

40 years ago, Planet Astra of the Olinian Galaxy, 20,345 light years away from Earth

He had to get away fast. They knew about his plan. His dirty blue robes trailed behind him as he ran, his black hair dishevelled.

The plan

He thought as he reached the barren spot of land.

There were no trees, no hills, no grass, just flat plain land as vast as the starry night sky.

He looked left and right to make sure no one was there.

He got his gun from the pack slung over his shoulder. It was an unusual contraption, a hunk of metal engraved with a foreign language, and from inside it came a ghostly green light. The most uncommon thing was that the gun wasn't created to shoot, instead for a purpose no human would have thought possible. In fact, this entire event is one thing that a mere human mind could never comprehend.

The man reached into his bag once more and came out with a large metal shovel. He started digging as fast as possible, careful to make sure no one heard him.

He continued his work till he reached a level of depth he thought sufficient. He charged up his gun, and was about to shoot, when a deep voice resonated from behind him. "You cannot leave. You must surrender to us."

The speaker of the voice was invisible.

"NEVER!" The man shouted, his voice unexpectedly shrill.

"Do not do this to me, son." The voice softened. A man with a stark white beard came into view. He was dressed in similar robes.

"You were never my father."

"You have to listen to me! Your siblings need you. Especially Aya. If you surrender, they won't come for you!"

His expression softened for a second but then returned to its usual anger. "If you were really my father, you'd try to stop them."

"I have tried reasoning with you, Azul. But now, it is not in my hands. Goodbye, my son."

Azul fired his gun at the chasm and jumped in.

"I told you he would run away like a coward, Father." A young woman came into view, her dark brown hair was tied up into an elegant bun and she wore a light blue dress. Her eyes smouldered with defiance and anger.

The old man sighed. "Looks like you were right, Aria."

"Of course, Father. Now, who shall we send from our army to destroy him?"

"*My* army and you mean *capture* him." The old man corrected.

Aria rolled her eyes. "Yes, yes, as you say."

"Good. Go tell your siblings to come here immediately."

"But, Father, surely I can do–"

"Who is the General here, Aria?"

"You, Father."

"Then go do as I say or do you want me to force you?"

"Of course not, Father." She turned and briskly walked away.

Aria strutted back to the camp they had set up in the middle of the desert. Aria never liked her father's ways. She hated how much hope he had for Azul. Aria then decided to enact the plans, which were brewing in her head for months. If she killed that stupid old man, she could become the General of the Astran Army, who had complete control of the planet.

Her plan sent a thrill up her spine. She thought of a way to murder him. She realised that she can sneak into the weapon facility and get the prototype guns they were storing there. She snuck in unnoticed and stole one of the flammable guns which were made for stealth missions

She then ran back to where her father was waiting.

"Aria! Where are the others? What are you doing here? Did you forget the-"

His interrogation was cut short when Aria got the gun from a pocket in her dress. She aimed at her father's heart but ended up shooting right next to his heart. Astran bullets were extremely effective compared to other planets, so even a shot in their chest can lead to death.

She threw the gun to the floor and lit it with a match. Her eyes were manic in the firelight.

"Why? Aria?" Her father stammered his last words. "How could you?" His body lay motionless on the sandy ground, his eyes staring aimlessly at the constellations.

"Goodbye, Father. May your soul burn in hell!" Aria said.

She waited till the fire died down and picked up the ashes and scattered them. She then scooped her father's body into her hands. She ran back to camp and fake-cried "Oh no, Father, FATHER!" She shook him.

Her siblings came running towards her. A young man with the same dark hair and a young girl no more than six.

"Aria, What happened?" The young man asked.

"Oh, Anel," Aria sniffled. "Azul killed Father in his rage and escaped with his portal gun." She broke down in tears after she told him a story that was so believable, you'd have believed it yourself.

The little girl hugged herself. "No, no, no! Brother Azul would never do that! He might have not liked Father but he isn't a murderer!" She broke down in tears.

Anel pulled his younger sister close.

Their father's right hand man, Arol, coming running towards them. "WHAT IS THIS TREACHERY?!" He yelled.

"Azul killed Father." Anel said icily. His voice was strangely calm, as if he could see right through Aria's act.

"What? Send a search party out for him right now! We will not rest until he's dead!" Arol ordered.

Aria put her hands to her mouth to hide her smirk.

Everything worked out exactly to plan, I am the oldest without Azul, I will now be the General!

"Oh no! Who will be the General if Azul and Father are gone?" Aria asked.

"I presume it would be you, Aria, Your father put you next in line after Azul." Arol said.

"I will go put Aya to sleep." Anel said and walked away with his sister in tow. He knew Aria's plan, he also knew that he could stop her. But.......*Maybe her idea isn't so bad*...He'll regret this choice in the future.

"Bye Anel." She said in a sombre tone but only *those* words were sombre ones, "All right then, My first order would be to gather all our forces to find and kill Azul."

"Yes, miss but-"

"It's *General* now, Arol, go do what I say or do you want me to force you?" She said in a harsh tone as she got up from her knees and wiped her hands on her blue dress.

"No, General." Arol saluted and walked away.

Chapter 1
THE EXPEDITION

Present day, Planet Astra of the Olinian Galaxy, 20,345 million light years away from Earth, Loyan Island, The Xanner Estate.

"Alera!" A woman with chocolate brown hair and beautiful green eyes called, searching the crystal palace for her daughter. "Where did that girl go?"

"I'm right here, Mother!" Alera called.

Her mother ran towards the voice of her daughter,

"Hello!" Alera said brightly. She was dressed in her usual blue button up dress and dark trousers. Her dark brown hair spilled over her shoulders, looking uncannily like her mother's, though she had her father's pale blue eyes. She seemed to be about 11 years old. "I'm almost 12 you know, I don't need my mother taking care of me."

"Alera! COME HERE NOW!" An angry voice bellowed.

"Oh what have you done again?" Her mother muttered and dragged her daughter towards the voice.

Alera giggled "Nothing, Mother. "

They walked into a bedroom with a large king-sized bed and walls lined with bookshelves. Right in front of them in the doorway was Ayan, Alera's older brother, drenched in water.

"Oh, Alera! What did you do!?" Her mother said.

Alera feigned an innocent expression.

Her mother sighed and helped Ayan clean up.

Why did I have to have such a difficult child? She thought somberly as she dried Ayan's hair.

"At least now you don't need a bath." Alera said.

Ayan growled at her.

"Children, please." Their mother said. "The twins were never this much trouble!"

"But we're not the twins!" They both said at once, this was the only thing they could agree on.

Alera and Ayan had other siblings, Ayun and Asaya. Both left for college two years ago and were perfect children with spotless rooms and straight As, their parents kept comparing them with Asaya and Ayun, 'Why are your grades so bad?" They would say to Alera. "Asaya never had such bad grades when she was younger!"

"Father is going to be back tomorrow." Their mother said, "Clean your rooms and dress in your best clothes. That includes you too, Alera."

"Yes, mother, I will, I will." Alera rolled her eyes.

Her mother sighed. "Ok, I think you both should get working on your rooms." She walked out of Ayan's bedroom.

She went into her own room and shut the door. She sank to the floor. She whispered something to herself and a single tear leaked down her left cheek.

"Are you reading a book about EarthLings?" Alera asked him.

"YES! Can't you see the title? Earth and its beings. And they aren't called EarthLings, they're called humans. Would you like it if a human calls you an AstraLing instead of an Ironan?"

"Actually, I wouldn't mind."

"Just leave me alone, will you?"

"Fine. I will." She said and trotted back to her room.

She roamed around her room aimlessly and searched for something to do. When she found that nothing was available, she flopped onto her bed and sighed.

Then an idea came to her mind, one so obviously wrong she couldn't wait to try it, she knew her mother would murder her for this but,

What's the fun in life if you don't take risks? She thought.

She got out her bag and packed a few essentials.

I think I should do it at night, when everyone is asleep.

Alera had dinner quickly, trying to look inconspicuous. She waited until the sun set. In Astra the sun appeared to be blue, so every sunset would look like an abstract painting of the oceans of Earth.

She waited till the four moons and the stars were visible and crept out of her room. As she noiselessly walked around her house she passed her brother's room, the door was only open a crack but enough to see inside, Alera peeked into her brother's room and found him weeping on the bed.

"What in the world?" She whispered aloud.

She opened the door and burst into his room, giving next to zero respect for his privacy.

"Alera?!" Ayan asked, startled and confused. "Wha-what are you doing there? D-did you see that?"

"Ayan! Why were you crying?"

"So you *did* see that. I won't tell you unless you tell me why you were spying on me."

"I wasn't spying on you!"

"Really? You *were not* setting up another prank?"

"NO! Of course not!"

"Prove it."

Alera sighed "I was going to leave the island to explore."

"ARE YOU CRAZY?"

"Only for a little while! I wanted to see what it was like outside. I'd be back by dawn! Now that I said what I was doing. What were *you* doing?"

It was Ayan's turn to sigh. "I was reading a book."

"You were crying because of a book? Never mind, I don't wanna know."

"Now go back to sleep." Ayan said.

"Nope. I'm gonna go to Sirriea"

"What? No! No, you are not!"

Alera jumped out of the window and ran.

"Oh why!!" Ayan said and followed her.

He had to run quite a lot to catch up with her. "Alera! Where are you-"

Before he could finish she ran even faster and eventually reached the beach. There was one ship left, it was a cargo boat set for Saaz, the capital of Sirrea.

Ayan had no choice but to jump after her. The ship started moving and Alera and Ayan ducked behind a box.

"Alera! How are we going to go back?" Ayan whispered.

She shrugged.

Ayan cursed.

"Wow, you know some *colourful* words." Alera muttered.

They kept quiet for the rest of the trip, finally the ship reached its destination. They both hopped out and ducked behind a tree.

"Great, now what do we do?" Ayan asked.

"Explore!" Alera said and sprinted into the woods.

"Aghhhh! Not again." Ayan muttered and followed her.

They passed through the woods, and surprisingly the deeper they went, the sparser it became, finally they reached a spot of dry land surrounded by a barbed fence . The sign said,

WARNING! RADIOACTIVE ☢

Authorised by the General of the Astran Army

Alera jumped right over the fence.

"Oh Lord of Astra!" Ayan exclaimed. "I'm not gonna go through! I'm not gonna go through! Nope, I can't break the law."

"Ayan, you've gotta come here!" Alera called.

Ayan sighed. He braced himself and jumped, having no other choice and caring too much about his sister's safety to do otherwise.

He was going to fall. *I'm such an idiot.* He thought

But surprisingly something cushioned his fall.

Groaning noises came from underneath him.

Then he realised that he must have fallen on top of Alera. He scrambled off her and offered his hand. "I'm so sorry, Alera, I didn't mean to. But for the record, I think you deserved that for running away from the house."

"It's okay, I think I broke my back." She said, "Anyways, there's the thing I called you here for." She pointed towards a large chasm in the middle of the clearing. They ran towards it.

"We shouldn't be here." Ayan said.

Alera rolled her eyes. "Of course you think that, brother."

"I think that because it's the right way to think."

"There is no 'right way' to think- never mind. Come on, let's see what's down there."

"What?! NO"

She slid down the chasm.

"Well, too late." Ayan sighed and slid down beside her, this time careful not to land on her back.

"Whoa." Alera said, her eyes fixed on the small green hole in the middle of the chasm.

"What the heck is that?"

"Let's take a closer look."

"You know what, this time I'm not even going to try to talk you out of it."

They both came closer to the emerald crater.

"This is so cool." Alera said.

"I actually agree with you for once."

She peered into the pit. Ayan followed her out of curiosity.

Suddenly, they were sucked into the ditch. That was both the worst and the best thing that had ever happened to them.

Chapter 2
THE KIDS WHO FELL FROM THE SKY

3 days later, Planet Earth of the Milky Way Galaxy, India, Hyderabad, Kukatpally

Aakriti was having a usual day,

She woke up to her alarm, changed into her school uniform and asked her mother to comb her thick black hair into two plaits. She was almost eleven years old and went to a decent school. Her mother gave her breakfast, and she walked to the bus stop and climbed her bus. She searched for her best friend in the crowd, Priya. She was sitting at the front and was saving a seat for her. Priya wore her hair in a braid and had skin the colour of coffee. Aakriti walked towards her and greeted her with their usual handshake, clap-clap fist bump and high-five. Sitting behind them was their other friend, Devesh.

"Hey, guys." He said.

"Hey," Priya said to Devesh. She turned towards Aakriti. Her brown eyes wide. "Did you know that Preetha is *not* coming to school today? That's like the best news since I found out that I got into the cricket team!"

Preetha Sharma was the bully of the school, she was always picking on Aakriti and her friends.

"Really? That's great." Aakrti said as she took her seat beside Priya.

"Why are you guys so afraid of that girl?" Devesh asked them.

"We could ask the same question about Raj." Aakriti said to Devesh.

"Well, he's the captain of the cricket team and he *always* picks on me. Plus he's, like, 8th grade!" He said.

"It's the same reason for us!"Priya said.

"Fine, So, want to hang out after cricket practice?" Devesh put his chin on the back of their seat.

"When does the boys' cricket practice end?" Aakriti asked.

"At around 4:30."

"Cool. Ours ends by 4."Priya said.

"So my house at 5?" Aakriti said.

"Ok." Devesh said.

Aakriti reached into her school bag and got out a novel.

"Oh, come on, Kriti! You always read on the bus! Can't you just *talk* to us for once?" Priya protested.

"I'm in such a good part!! The main character literally dies! I need to know if he lives!" Aakriti retorted.

"Why would you read a book if the main character dies in it?" Devesh asked dubiously.

"Because it's interesting!" She said,

He snatched the book from her hands and held it above his head.

"Hey!"

He tossed it to Priya.

She put it above her head since she was taller than me. "Na na na na na!"

"Come on! That's not fair!"Aakriti stood up and plucked the book from her hands.

"NO STANDING ON THE BUS!" The bus helper yelled in Telugu.

Everyone turned towards her. She could feel her cheeks flushing with embarrassment.

"Sorry." She said and settled back into her seat.

"This is all your fault!" Aakriti hissed at Devesh.

"My fault?! Priya could have given it back to you!"

They both turned towards Priya. "What? Don't look at me!"

Then suddenly the bus stopped.

They all got down the bus and walked to their classes. Priya and Aakriti were in the same class. They both said bye to Devesh and walked to their classroom.

Their teacher was Deepika ma'am.

She started explaining something when Aakriti opened her novel underneath her desk and started reading.

"Aakriti!!" Deepika ma'am yelled. "What is the answer to this problem?"

"Uh . . ." She looked at the board. The problem was a crossword of brackets and symbols with numbers thrown around in the middle.

RING-RING!!! The bell sounded.

Saved by the bell. Aakriti thought.

Deepika ma'am glared at her "Today's homework is complete exercise 1B…" She wrote on the blackboard

The next class was science, they had a combined class with 6D, Devesh's section.

Jyothi ma'am, their science teacher, entered the room.

Everyone in the class greeted her with a namaste.

Behind their science teacher class 6D entered, and all of them shared a seat with one of the students. Devesh sat beside Dhanush, his best friend.

As soon as everyone settled down, Jyothi ma'am told us to open our science textbooks. We were in the lesson Sources of Food.

Unexpectedly, The vice principal entered the room. Everyone in the class stood up and said, "Namaste ma'am."

The vice principal said in her booming voice, "School is cancelled today." She said, "Wait for your class teacher to arrive and then you can leave. The reason will be disclosed to your parents in an email."

Everyone managed to keep neutral expressions till the teachers left.

"YESS!!" One person yelled and pumped his fist. "TODAY'S A FRIDAY! NO HOMEWORK THE WHOLE WEEKEND!!!"

"Why are we all waiting here?! LET'S GO!" Dhanush said

"We should wait till Archana ma'am comes back.." Devesh said.

"Nah, lets just go, anyways, Archana ma'am isn't our class teacher."

Few people in the class, including Aakriti, Priya and Devesh, walked out of the room and went to their buses.

They climbed in and took their usual seats.

There were only 2 other people in the bus. The bus driver was yet to come from his breakfast break.

"So…Is your elder sister back from her 'esteemed robotics science program'" Devesh asked Priya.

"Nope. She's gonna stay there for like another 15 days. 2 weeks of all the Netflix and Coke to myself. It seems like a dream." Priya said.

"You're lucky. My parents don't even allow me to watch Netflix or drink Coke." Devesh said.

"Wow. That's sad." Priya said.

Slowly everyone entered the bus, the last person to enter was the bus driver.

"PLEASE BE QUIET!" He yelled to the eighth graders in Telugu and started the bus.

Devesh was frozen in his seat.

"Hey, Devesh!?" Aakriti waved a hand in front of his face.

He just pointed towards one of the eighth graders. Aakriti didn't recognize him at first and then realised that he was pointing towards Raj.

"Why is Raj on our bus?" Priya asked, confused.

"I heard he moved recently." Aakriti replied

"Don't be such a scaredy-cat!" Priya said to Devesh, who was trying to hide his face with his jacket's hood.

"Don't talk so loudly!" Devesh hissed.

"We're lucky my house is the first stop." Aakriti said.

"Oh no." Devesh ducked behind his bag. "He spotted me."

"It's okay, Devesh. It's not like Raj will kill you. I mean, sure he's a really bad bully and picks on everyone and he *is in eighth* grade but it's not like- he's right behind me isn't he?" Priya said.

“Yes.” Aakriti said to her.

“So I’m a bully, eh? You wanna be bullied?” Raj said to Priya.

“Sure. I don’t mind.” Priya said.

“What is wrong with you?” Aakriti asked her.

“What is wrong with you? I never understood why Devesh was so afraid of him.”Priya said.

“Ok. fine.” Aakriti agreed..

Raj walked away.

“See? If you don’t let the bully bully you, they won’t.”Priya said.

“Oh no.” Aakriti said.

Raj came back with two of the most muscular 8th graders.

The bus stopped by the stop they climbed on just 1 hour ago.

“Finally.” Priya said

Priya, Devesh and Aakriti left the bus and walked to Aakriti’s house.

“That was a close call.” Devesh said.

“Yeah. Sure was.” Aakriti said.

They reached Aakriti’s house and opened the door to find Aakriti’s Amma looking very surprised.

“Hey, sweetie. Priya, Devesh.” Her Amma said.

"Hi, Auntie." Priya said.

"Why are you guys here so early?" Aakriti's Amma, Aishwarya, looked confused.

"We don't know, the teachers suddenly said school was cancelled." Devesh explained.

"Do you mind if they stay in my room?" Aakriti asked Amma.

"Sure. They can stay till lunch." Her Amma said.

"Thanks, Amma." Aakriti kissed her mother on the cheek and everyone went up to her room.

"So, could you guys like, wait outside till I change?" Aakriti asked them

"Sure."

"Ok."

Aakriti changed from her school uniform to a white top and black jeans. "Come in!"

Devesh and Priya came into the room.

"So, you guys have to see Unlisted on Netflix, It's awesome. There's this other movie on Disney called Spin.."

"I'd love to see them if my parents allowed me to use Netflix!" Devesh said.

"I can see the Netflix one but I don't have Disney plus. If you want, Devesh, we can go see the series right now. I mean, my parents allow me to watch Netflix." Aakriti said.

"Hey, Aakriti. The sky over there looks really dark. I think it's gonna rain." Priya said.

They all turned to look at the window and gasped when they saw a green portal open right above them and watched as a little girl with dark hair landed in their backyard. Right after her came a guy with the same features, who fell on top of her.

"Oh my god!!" Aakriti exclaimed.

"I'm not going crazy right? You can see them too???" Devesh asked.

"Yes, Devesh. We can see them too but that could just mean we all are going crazy." Priya said.

"Let's go!" Aakriti said.

"What do you mean? We're not gonna go there!" Devesh said. "Have you gone crazy?!" He said in telugu.

"Yeah we are! They're in my backyard!" Aakriti said.

"Oh no.." Devesh said as they all left the room and walked out of the house.

"I feel like saying a word I'm definitely not supposed to say." Priya said.

"Where are you guys going?" Aishwarya, Aakriti's Amma, asked.

"Just to the backyard. To play some cricket. We don't have practice today as school got cancelled." Aakriti said and went to the backyard.

"You lied to your mother!" Devesh whispered.

"Yeah, so? It's not a big deal. I always lie to my mother about doing my homework." Priya said.

Devesh shook his head.

They reached the backyard.

Chapter 3
THE YELLOW STAR

Present day, Planet Earth of the Milky Way Galaxy, India, Hyderabad, Kukatpally

Alera and Ayan tumbled through the green void for who knows how long. Ayan was screaming the whole time, which annoyed Alera to a great extent.

Finally, they landed on a small grassy plain behind a big box-like structure made out of bricks.

Alera landed down on her feet and suddenly, Ayan landed on top of her.

Alera pushed Ayan off of her. "IF YOU DO THAT ONCE MORE! I SWEAR TO THE LORD OF ASTRA THAT I WILL PUNCH YOU IN THE FACE!"

"Ok, I won't." Ayan said.

"Where are we, anyways? The sun is so yellow, this is definitely not Astra." Alera said, squinting at the unusual sun.

"Yes, this is not Astra. I think we're on Earth."

"What?! No way! That's like a million light years away!!"

"Yeah but this place matches the description of Earth in the book I was reading. Yellow sun, box houses, very green grass."

"Those things are houses?! How can EarthLings live in those ?"

Behind a bush, Aakriti, Devesh and Priya were listening to their conversation.

"OMG! They're aliens!" Priya whispered.

"This could just be a prank." Devesh pointed out.

"If it is a prank, it would be really hard to make that portal look real." Aakriti said.

"Yeah..or we all have gone crazy." Priya said.

"That's a possibility." Devesh said.

"One of us should go and talk to them." Priya said.

"Yeah." Aakriti agreed.

They both turned towards Devesh. "What?"

Priya pushed him out of the bush.

"Hey!" Devesh said to Priya.

Alera and Ayan turned towards the noise.

"Oooo! EARTHLINGS!! THIS IS SOO COOL!!!" Alera said. "HELLO! MY NAME IS A-L-E-R-A . I AM FROM ASTRA AND AN IRONAN"

"I'm sorry about my sister. I don't know what is the right way to greet humans. I didn't complete the etiquette chapter in the book Earth and its beings. My name is Ayan and we are from the planet Astra of the Olinian Galaxy" Ayan said and bowed.

"Uh..." Devesh said. "Guys, I don't think these people are fakes." He said to the bush.

"Okay. So humans talk to bushes to greet people." Ayan nodded as if he understood why.

Priya and Aakriti came from behind the bush.

"Ooooo! MORE EARTHLINGS!! NICE TO MEET YOU ALL!" Alera yelled.

"We are on Earth, right?" Ayan asked.

"Yes..." Aakriti dragged out the word.

"Where are you from??! Who are your parents? Are you really aliens?? WHO ARE YOU?! What are you doing in Aakriti's backyard? Did you-" Priya was interrupted by Aakriti. "Priya, you need to breathe."

Priya took a deep breath. "How'd you get the portal illusion? Did you create it yourself? Are you from the USA? Can you-"

"Priya!" Devesh and Aakriti said in unison.

"Ok, fine. I'll stop." Priya said.

"So, who sent you here? " Aakriti said.

"WE CAME HERE BY ACCIDENT!" Alera shouted.

"Alera, Humans might have much less hearing capacity than us but it doesn't mean that they're deaf." Ayan said.

"I KNOW!" Alera said loudly.

"Then please lower your voice." Ayan begged.

"Ok, sorry. I get a little excited when I'm somewhere new." Alera said.

"Wait, so you never came to Hyderabad before this?" Priya asked.

"No, not really. What is Hyderabad? We've never been to Earth." Ayan said.

"Ok, soo, let's take you inside so we can question you more." Priya said.

"Yeah." Devesh agreed.

"It's my house! My Amma won't let me get two random kids in!" Aakriti protested.

"I'm not a kid! In fact, I probably am older than you, my sister is 11 and I'm 12." Ayan said.

Aakriti, Devesh and Priya ignored Ayan and started arguing among themselves. Finally, they came to a conclusion that they would say the school sent Ayan and Alera as exchange students from a different place.

"Ok, let's go into our house." Priya said.

"*My* house." Aakriti corrected.

Ayan and Alera trailed behind them. When they entered the house, Aishwarya looked up from the pasta she was making. "Aakriti, who are these kids? I thought you went to play cricket."

"Oh, the school just sent these kids for an exchange program. They said that they sent you an email and that you approved." Aakriti said.

"Yeah. . . an *email* and you *did* approve. I saw you do it." Devesh said.

Aakriti wanted to slap her forehead or Devesh but that would give her away.

"Devesh, just shut up and let us do the talking." Priya said from the side of her mouth. Then she laughed nervously. "Oh, Devesh, your jokes are so funny! Ha, ha ha!"

"We're just gonna take them up to my room." Aakriti said and they all hurried up the stairs.

"But-Oh well." Aishwarya, her mother said.

They all crowded into Aakriti's bedroom. Priya shut the door.

"So. . . I'm going to ask you a few questions and you should give honest answers." Priya got out a rough notebook and pen from Aakriti's bookshelf.

"Ok." Alera was peering out the window and straight at the sun.

"Sure!" Ayan said cheerfully.

"Where are you from?" Priya asked.

"We are from Planet Astra of the Olinian Galaxy." Ayan said.

"It orbits a blue star and is, like, a million light years away from Earth. I don't know how that stupid portal got us here." Alera said.

"So you are aliens?" Priya asked.

"If you call Ironans aliens." Alera said.

"What are Ironans?" Devesh thought aloud.

"Ironans are the species we are. Like humans." Ayan said.

"Or Yuvanans." Alera added.

"Yuvu-what now?" Aakriti said.

"They're another species. They have a very smart mind and can take over the universe if they want. But they don't. Because if they do, the Ironans and Humans from other planets will lock them up, every species has an Achilles' heel. " Ayan said.

"I have to go to the bathroom." Priya excused herself from the room.

"I thought that was a Greek phrase. And isn't Greece on Earth?" Devesh asked.

"It is on Earth but the Greek Empire didn't originate on Earth, I think a Martian started the Greek Empire on Earth. Now, there is another planet called Greece, where the people are descended from the great Greek heroes of every planet, they say the Olympians walk their land. Even Astra, our planet, had its Greek heroes." Ayan explained.

"Whoa." Devesh exclaimed.

"You know he could be making all that up, right?" Priya said.

"But it's still super cool." Devesh argued. "And if he is making it up, he has one heck of an imagination."

"Thank you?" Ayan said uncertainly.

Suddenly, Alera fainted.

Ayan caught her.

"What happened to her?" Devesh asked.

Ayan eased her onto Aakriti's bed. "I think she got dehydrated or something because of looking at the yellow sun. Could you go get me some water?"

"Ok, she's fine right?" Aakriti asked.

"She will be if you get me some water." Ayan said.

Aakriti walked down the stairs and grabbed a glass of water. "Here." She said to Ayan.

Ayan poured some water into Alera's mouth and splashed some water on her face. She gasped and woke up."WHY'D YOU DO THAT?!"

"Oh, I'm sorry, I just caught you when you fainted and got you awake. So scream at me, no 'thank you, Ayan'" Ayan said.

"Ugh. Fine. Thank you, Ayan." Alera said.

"You're welcome." Ayan said.

Priya came back from the restroom. "Did I miss something?" She looked at all of their faces.

"Nope. Nothing." Devesh lied.

"So, I'm going to continue my questions." Priya sat down. "Ok, how did you guys find the portal that sent you to Earth?"

"That's quite a long story, actually." Ayan said.

Chapter 4
THE MISSING CHILDREN

Present day, Planet Astra of the Olinian Galaxy, 20,345 million light years away from Earth, General Aria's base

General Aria was pacing around her base, she was in a bad mood, which explained why she lashed out at the messenger who came to her with surprisingly useful news.

"General, I-" The messenger was saying.

"Shh. I must think." Aria held up a hand.

"But, General, this might-"

"What did I say?"

"Yes, General."

The messenger walked out and reported back to Arol. "Sir, the General is not listening."

"Then I shall go talk to her myself." Arol said and walked to Aria.

"General, There is important news." Arol said firmly.

Aria sighed. " Yes, Arol."

"Your sister's children, Aya's children, have gone missing."

"So? She deserves it for refusing to be here."

"But, guess where they were seen last?"

"Near the Xanner Estate?"

"No, near the Chasm."

That got Aria's attention. "What, they were near the portal?"

"Yes."

"Aya sent her children to find Azul before me? Oh, no, She thinks her children can find Azul faster than my ENTIRE ARMY?! Send a team into the Chasm right now. We need to find Azul. And capture those pesky kids if you find them. We already took two of her children for the army. Can't we take the other two?"

"Yes, General." Arol walked out.

"Oh, no, Ajdin! The authorities have said that our children are not anywhere on Loyan!" Aelia sobbed.

"It's all right, Loyan is a very big island, they will be somewhere on it. If they are not here, we can start searching the coast of Sirriea." Adjin said calmly, he was actually bursting with worry on the inside but he knew he had to be strong for his wife. "If the authorities don't find our children, my crew and I will start searching for them. Right now, you need to eat and rest. You've barely slept for the past three days"

"All right." Aelia said. Ajdin led Aelia into the dining room.

"So let me get this straight," Priya said. "You didn't listen to your mother, left your house, climbed a boat, went to the mainland, passed a sign that said 'DANGER, RADIOACTIVE', ended up going into a weird chasm-portal greenish thingy and landed in our backyard."

"*My* backyard." Aakriti corrected.

Priya waved her off. "We stay here more than our houses."

"Yes. That is exactly what happened." Ayan said with a straight face.

"Wow! This is like the beginning of a sci-fi adventure series!" Priya said.

"Or could just be a made-up lie from Preetha." Devesh said.

"Wow, way to kill the mood, Devesh." Priya said

"It's all my fault we're here." Alera said from the bed. "I should be doing something to get us back to Astra."

"You need to rest, the sun has dehydrated you very much." Ayan said.

"Wait, if you're aliens, why do you speak English? Shouldn't you speak your own language?" Devesh asked.

"You see, English isn't only popular on Earth, another species made the language in the planet Hoaral of the Demexar Galaxy and it slowly made its way to Earth and many other planets." Ayan explained.

"So wait, every single big breakthrough on Earth is from aliens?" Devesh asked.

"Yes, I think so." Ayan said.

"So,what, are Albert Einstein and Nicola Tesla aliens?" Aakriti asked.

"I believe Nicola Tesla was a human and Albert Einstein was an Ironan." Ayan said thoughtfully. "Human minds aren't usually as powerful as Ironans."

"GREAT! We'll probably find out that Marie Curie was an alien too." Aakriti said.

"Yes, I think she was Saturnian." Ayan said, not knowing that Aakriti was being sarcastic.

"Ugh!!" Aakriti stormed out.

"Did I do something wrong?" Ayan asked obliviously.

"Nope, you did nothing wrong!" Priya said. "Just gave me a topic for my English writing homework!! It was due today but I was so lucky that school got cancelled! I have like two days to complete it."

"Should I call Aakriti back here?" Devesh asked.

"Why?" Priya said.

"You're her best friend! You should be offering!" Devesh said.

"Fine! I'll call her back." Priya went out of the room.

"I'm hungry, does Earth have lunch?" Alera asked.

"Sure. Let's go to Auntie." Devesh said.

Devesh led Alera and Ayan out of the room. They passed Priya and Aakriti conversing, finally, Aakriti grudgingly nodded, Priya and Aakriti joined the others.

"So, why are you here?" Aakriti asked. "I thought Alera needed to rest."

"I'm hungry." She said,

"Oh, I think my Amma's done with the pasta for lunch." Aakriti said.

"What is pasta?" Ayan asked.

"Oh my gosh, you don't know what pasta is? Pasta is the best lunch food on Earth!" Aakriti explained enthusiastically, "It's from this country named Italy."

Aakriti led Ayan and Alera to the Kitchen/Dining room.

"Looks like Aakriti is way more willing to help now." Devesh said to Priya. "What did you say to her?"

"I just reminded her how hard it was for me when I first moved back to India. She made it much easier then." Priya answered.

"Yes, you were so weird." Devesh said.

Priya swatted him. They both followed Aakriti and the Ironans.

"So, Amma, the *exchange students* are hungry, do you think you can give them some pasta?" Aakriti asked.

"Of course! Sweetie!" Auntie said and ladled some fusilli pasta onto plates and served them to everyone. "Sit down, sit down."

"Wow, this pasta thing sure tastes great!" Alera said.

"Yeah, it does." Ayan agreed.

"I never catched your names, if you'll be living in our house, it's better I know them." Auntie said.

"Oh, my name is Al-" Alera was interrupted by Aakriti. "-lisa. Alisa Smith. Yup, that's her name."

"No, my name is Ale-" She tried again.

"Hahahaha! You're so funny." Devesh laughed nervously.

Everyone turned towards him, Devesh hated being the centre of attention. "Why are you looking at me?"

"Ok... what is your name?" Auntie asked Ayan, he wasn't as dumb as Alera to say his Ironan name, he knew from reading his fact books that Earth was one of the 500 planets that didn't know about extraterrestrial life. So he said "My name is Ryan Smith. Me and Aler- I mean Alisa are siblings."

"Oh, so where are you from?" Auntie asked.

Why is my Amma so curious!? Can't she just not ask questions!? Aakriti thought and groaned inwardly.

"They're from...uh... California!" Aakriti lied.

"Which city, and let them answer this time, Aakriti, I know you like talking but they should be allowed to talk too." Her Amma said.

"No really, we would love it if Aakriti answers!!" Ayan or now Ryan said.

"It's okay, you do know English." Auntie laughed. "So what's the name of the city? I might know someone there."

"Uh..um ... .it's...The Island of Loyaan! It's very small, so you wouldn't know it." Alera/Alisa said.

"Ok...I didn't know the school there had an exchange program. It sounds like a remote island" Auntie said.

"Yes..." Alera said, clueless to what she was agreeing too.

"I THINK ALISA AND RYAN WANT TO SEE TV!" Devesh said loudly.

"Yes... we do?" Alera/Alisa said.

"COME ON!" Devesh yelled and dragged them to the living room.

Priya facepalms. "He is so bad at lying." She muttered.

Chapter 5
THE 'HUMAN' SCHOOL

2 days later, Planet Earth of the Milky Way Galaxy, India, Hyderabad, Kukatpally

It was an exhausting weekend. The whole time, she had to stop Alera and Ayan, sorry, *Alisa* and *Ryan* from breaking everything in the house.

The evening on which they arrived, they thought tiny people were stuck in the TV, they almost broke it with a vase her mother bought in an antique store.

On Saturday, *Alisa* thought a landline phone was a fire alarm and that a Barbie doll was a scary mind-control machine. *Ryan* ended up reading every book in her bookshelf. He even colour-coded them and arranged them in fattest to thinnest. Not that organising her stuff was bad, that just meant she didn't have to clean her room for at least another month, but she didn't want some weird-alien person digging through all her stuff.

And Sunday was the worst of them all, her Amma wanted to take *Alisa* and *Ryan* to the movies! There was this new marvel movie screening, The Eternals, she was forced to watch the movie instead of playing cricket with Priya and Devesh. The movie wasn't even nice! On top of all of that, Alera, sorry, I mean *Alisa* kept on scaring the people in front of them. *Ryan* kept stealing popcorn from Aakriti's bowl. He was addicted to it!

Finally, the movie was over by 11 pm, and they went home. Her Amma said that she had to give her room to *Alisa* and *Ryan.* She had to sleep in the living room!

That Monday morning, she woke up to her alarm clock ringing. Her neck throbbed from sleeping on the sofa set. She got her alarm from her room and put it on the coffee table in front of the couch. It was around seven am, her bus arrived at eight-thirty. She crept up the stairs and tip-toed to her room. *Alisa* and *Ryan* were still sleeping. She walked into the restroom and showered. She changed into the school uniform and came out.

Aakriti walked over to *Alisa* and shaked her. She just groaned and turned in her sleeping bag beside Aakriti's bed, in which *Ryan* was restfully sleeping.

"ALERA!" Aakriti said in her ear.

Alera, aka, *Alisa* sat up straight. "What time is it? Where are we?"

"You are in my house. I am Aakriti, the 'Earthling'. Remember?" Aakriti said.

"Oh, I thought all that was just a dream. . . ."

"It wasn't, and now you have to attend school so my Amma won't find it suspicious. Put this on." Aakriti gave *Alisa* a pair of her school uniform.

She went to the bathroom and changed.

"So. . . what do I do now?" *Alisa* or Alera asked.

Aakriti fanned the air. "Maybe brush your teeth? Your breath smells like dirty socks in fish stew."

"Ok. Could you lend me your toothbrush?" Alisa asked.

"I'll just go and get you a spare one." Aakriti said and walked down.

Ryan groaned on the bed. "What time is it?"

"Ayan, wake up. We have to go to human school!! This is gonna be so fun!!" *Alisa* said.

"Here's your toothbrush." Aakriti handed *Alisa* a spare toothbrush. *Alisa* walked to the sink and started brushing her teeth.

"Let me phone Devesh and ask him for one of his uniforms." Aakriti said and climbed down the stairs.

She called Devesh and asked him. "WHY?!" He asked, startled.

"For *Ryan*." She said,

"Oh, I'll be right there."

Devesh came to her house with the uniform.

"Why do you need Devesh's school uniform?" Auntie asked from the kitchen, she was making french toast for breakfast.

"For Ryan!" Aakriti called to her.

"I thought the school would provide uniforms for them." She said,

"Um...their parents can't afford to buy them." Aakriti lied.

"Oh. That's sad." Her Amma said.

"I'll go give these to Ryan." Devesh said and went up the stairs.

"So, when do your exams start, sweetie?" Her Amma asked

Aakriti groaned "Not until after Christmas break, Amma."

"Oh, good, then you have the whole break to study Hindi with your father." Her Amma said.

"But it's the holidays!" Aakriti protested

"Yes, but it's also the only time your father is home. His business trips are always so long." Her mother looked wistful.

"We're getting late. There's like ten minutes till the bus arrives." Aakriti said, knocking her mother out of her memories.

Alisa walks down the stairs. "Is my breath better now?"

"Yes, but- oh well, come on!" Aakriti said.

Ryan and Devesh walked down behind her.

"Am I wearing this right?" *Ryan* asked, pointing to his necktie, which was stuffed into his pants' belt straps.

Devesh slapped his forehead. "No, you're not." He removed the tie from *Ryan's* pants and put it around his neck.

"Come on! We have to get to the bus stop." Aakriti said.

They all grabbed some french toast and walk out of the house.

"What is this thing? I absolutely love it!" *Alisa* said.

"It's French toast." Aakriti answered.

They reached the bus stop and sat on the waiting bench.

"Is 'french toast' from the same place as pasta?" Ryan asked.

"No, it's from France? I'm not exactly sure, since there are french fries but they are actually from Belgium." Devesh said.

"You're just confusing them more, Devesh." Aakriti told him.

Before Devesh could retort, the bus arrived and they all climbed on.

Aakriti sat in her usual place beside Priya, Devesh sat behind them and beside Devesh sat Alisa and Ryan.

"So, what is your 'school' like?" Ryan asked.

"You'll see." Priya said.

"Um, I don't know if this is rude, but I don't know your name," Ryan said to Priya.

"Oh, My name is Priya." She said, "And, no, it's not rude, I was the one who didn't introduce myself."

"Why are human names so weird? You put my human name as Alisa, What does that even mean?" Alisa thought out loud.

"So, do you think school will be normal today?" Devesh asked.

"I sure hope it will, if it isn't, it's just harder to make sure that these two here," Aakriti pointed her chin towards *Alisa* and *Ryan* "don't cause too much trouble, they almost broke the telephone and TV back home!"

"Well, this Christmas is sure gonna be an interesting one." Devesh said.

"We're Hindus, we don't celebrate Christmas." Priya asked,

"Anyone can celebrate Christmas!" Devesh protested.

"But-" Priya started

"Do you want me to tell you guys a pun? Cause' I would-" Aakriti started.

"NO!" Priya and Devesh said in unison.

"The answer will always be no to the question, Aakriti." Priya said.

"I want to listen to a pun! I know that it's a joke humans like, but we never had something like that on Astra." *Ryan* said.

"Yes!" Aakriti said, Priya and Devesh groaned. "Why did the scarecrow get promoted?"

"Uh...what's a 'scarecrow'?" *Alisa* asked.

"I think it's that mannequin thing humans put to scare birds away from their crops." *Ryan* said.

"Oh." *Alisa* said.

"But I don't get the pun." *Ryan* said.

"You didn't get to the good part yet, the answer is that the scarecrow was *outstanding in its field* ." Aakriti said.

"Uh…" Ryan said.

"Hahahaha!" Alisa tried for a laugh.

"You guys don't get it, do you?" Aakriti asked.

"Nope. We don't." Alisa admitted.

Aakriti sighed. "It's all right."

"The joke's really corny, though." Devesh said.

"I know! That's why I said that." Aakriti said.

"Does nobody really notice my face?!" Priya butted in.

Aakriti focused more closely on Priya's face. "You changed your hairstyle?" She tried.

"SERIOUSLY?" Priya said.

"Um. . ." Aakriti was blank.

"The spectacles, Aakriti! Can't you see those!? Maybe you need to get some too!" Priya pointed towards her new glasses, they had black frames and made her eyes look much bigger than they were.

"Oh, I didn't see that . . . sorry." Aakriti said.

"Um… why did you get them?" Devesh asked.

"I watched too much Netflix last night. I binge-watched the whole Unlisted series." Priya said.

"Well, I guess that's why my parents don't allow me to watch Netflix." Devesh looked out the window.

"Yeah, but I don't get the coke part." Priya said.

Suddenly, a sound like a car engine starting erupted from somewhere to my left.

Devesh snickered. "I guess that's why my parents don't allow coke."

Aakriti turned to find that Priya was the one who made that sound, who knew that she had such loud burps.

The noise sent many heads turning our way, their eyes drifted towards the new kids.

Murmurs and whispers ran around the bus.

"Hello!" Alisa said cheerily to one of them who turned to look at her.

"Hi. . ." The girl who turned said.

"What is your name?" Alisa asked.

"My name is Rhea." She said uneasily.

"Nice to meet you, Rhea!" Alisa offered her a hand.

They shook.

Rhea turned back. "She is so friendly." She whispered to someone sitting beside her.

"Uh…Alisa, I think it's best if you don't *interact* so much" Devesh told her.

"Ok..." Alisa pouted.

Chapter 6
THE NEW KIDS

Present day, 2 days later, Planet Earth of the Milky Way Galaxy, India, Hyderabad, Kukatpally

"What did I say about interacting?" Devesh chided Alisa after she greeted someone for the third time after they got out of the bus.

"Oh, come on! I just wanna say hello!" Alisa argued.

"Ugh!" Devesh groaned.

Priya snickered.

"What?" Devesh's head snapped towards Priya.

"Nothing…" Priya replied.

Devesh sighed, exasperated.

"Uh, guys? Preetha alert." Aakriti said.

"Is Preetha that other Earthling you were talking about ?" Alisa asked.

"Yes." Priya said.

"Wait, is that ... .is that Raj with Preetha?" Devesh ducked behind Ryan.

"What are you doing?" Ryan asked him.

"Raj." He whispered back.

"I thought he was just another student." Ryan said loudly.

"Be quiet!" He hissed.

"Ok, ok…" Ryan whispered.

Preetha and Raj came closer.

"Oh no." Aakriti said.

"Aakriti! Priya! Nice to see you both!!! HOW ARE YOU DOING!??" Preetha said.

"Wait, what? You're not gonna insult our bad way of dressing even though it's the school uniform, or tell us that we look horrible?" Priya asked sceptically.

Preetha laughed nervously "Oh why would I? YOU TWO ARE SO FUNNY!!"

"Uh. . . ." Aakriti said.

"Devesh!" Raj said. "Why are you hiding there, buddy?"

"Buddy?" Devesh mouthed. "Um. . . why are you being so nice…?" He asked Raj.

"So you're just gonna go straight up and ask him, when before you were so scared that you hid behind Ryan?" Priya folded her arms.

It was Devesh's turn to laugh nervously. "I wasn't scared."

"Uh, actually you were-" Priya was saying.

"SO! Why did the meatballs tell the spaghetti to go to sleep?" Aakriti said, trying to steer the conversation to a different topic.

"Uh. . .because the spaghetti was sleepy?" Preetha tried.

"Because it was pasta' bedtime," Aakriti said.

"HAHAHAHAHAHA!!!" Alisa laughed. " A PASTA JOKE!"

"Um....I don't want to be rude, but..uh...who are you?" Preetha asked.

"HELLO! I AM ALER- SORRY, ALISA!" Alisa yelled.

"I'm her brother, She is always so loud!" Ryan said. "By the way, my name is Ryan."

"Ok. . .are you the new students? Our teacher told us that a few new kids would be joining today..." Raj said.

Phew, we had enough luck! Aakriti thought

"Yes, yes they are!" She replied happily.

"But Alisa here looks way too young to be in seventh grade." Preetha said.

"That's because she's...she's a child prodigy!" Priya said, trying to cover up the fact that she was in fact, not a human student at all.

“Oh! That’s great news for our school!” Preetha said. “Well, now I have to go attend my first class, so goodbye!” She waved and walked away, Raj at her heels.

“So. . . what do you think that was about?” Priya asked.

“I have no idea. But we were lu-.” Aakriti was saying.

“Don’t jinx it.” Devesh interrupted.

“What’s a jinx?” Alisa asked.

“Right now, our main problem is making Alisa into a ‘child prodigy’.” Devesh said child prodigy with air quotes.

“Don’t worry.” Ryan said. “In Astra, we learn most things human 7th graders learn in Class 4. If she’s been paying attention in her school back home. Human school should be a breeze.”

“How do you know that? Wait, let me guess, you read it in a book.” Devesh said.

“Yes, I did!” Ryan said genuinely.

“Well, it looks like Ironans don’t understand sarcasm either.” Devesh muttered.

“What was that?” Ryan asked.

“Nothing.” Devesh said.

Priya snickered again.

“WHY DO YOU KEEP DOING THAT?” Devesh demanded.

That just made Priya laugh harder. Even Aakriti joined in.

"Ugh!" Devesh muttered something about having best friends who were girls.

"So, how does human school work?" Alisa asked as the group entered the school.

"You first have to find your locker, it's probably with the seventh graders," Priya said. "Though it will be hard to find since it's not supposed to have your name on it. And plus, no one will believe you're in the seventh grade, you look straight out of grade five."

"Um...after that?" Alisa asked.

"Actually, just scratch what I said before." Priya went to her locker and opened the door. "You just have to go to the administration block and they'll explain everything."

"Ok, could you take us there?" Ryan asked.

"Devesh will." Priya looked expectantly towards Devesh.

"What?" He said.

"You'll take Ryan and Alisa to the administration block?" Priya asked, though it was more like a demand, glaring at Devesh.

"Wait, wha-?" Devesh said, confused.

"Say yes." Aakriti whispered to him.

Devesh sighed. "Fine, I will."

"Good." Priya said.

Priya and Aakriti walked away towards their first class.

"So….where is this 'administration block'?" Alisa asked.

"It's right over there." Devesh pointed towards a staircase leading to the lower floors.

He guided Alisa and Ryan to the bottom floor which was the administration block. "Now, you have to go ask them where your class and locker is." Devesh said. He thought it was pretty straightforward and that they couldn't mess it up. So he waved them goodbye and left.

He reached his first class, which ended up being the same class as Priya and Aakriti.

This time, he decided not to ignore them when Priya called to him to sit beside them.

He walked over and sat behind Aakriti.

"Where are they?" Priya asked him.

Suddenly, someone walked into the room with their science teacher.

"Today, a new student will be joining us!" Ms. Patel said as someone who looked very familiar walked up behind her. "Alisa Smith!"

Chapter 7
THE FIRST DAY

Present day, 2 days later, Planet Earth of the Milky Way Galaxy, India, Hyderabad, Kukatpally

The whole science period, they had to stop Alisa from doing stupid things. She wasn't even supposed to be in seventh grade! She raised her hand so much that Ms. Patel had her stop and threatened that if she raised her hand one more time, she would go to detention, and that, of course, led to a long explanation about what detention was in the middle of class, which made them *get* detention.

Ugh! Aakriti thought. *Now AGAIN, because of Mr and Ms. ALIEN I can't play cricket! Well, at least some quiet time to read that book, Once Upon The End. And Devesh and Priya have to go through it with me.*

"AAKRITI!" Ms. Patel's voice shouted.

She snapped from her thoughts and said "Yes, ma'am?"

"What are the functions of blood?" Ms. Patterson asked.

"Uh…" Aakriti said. She knew the answer! She studied it with her mom!

Think, Aakriti! Think! She thought

"To give oxygen to all parts of the body?" She guessed.

"Correct!" Ms. Patterson said. "Now, Devesh, there's another point to the answer…"

Aakriti sighed inwardly.

The bell sounded.

'Okay, students! We have another science class after PE, so we'll continue this then!" Ms. Patel said.

They all emptied out the door, Priya, Aakriti and Alisa waved goodbye to Devesh.

The rest of the day at school went as a blur, they enjoyed their PE class and got to play some cricket, but then they had to explain the whole thing to Alisa. They met up with Ryan at lunch, "Human schools are extremely easy!" He had said. "I answered every question right and reorganised the classroom."

They all tried their best to stay away from Preetha and Raj but ended up bumping into them after detention, which made them miss cricket practice.

"Hello!" Preetha said brightly.

"Hi." Aakriti waved.

"HEY!" Alisa yelled.

"So, Alisa, that was your name right?" Preetha said. She nodded.

"So, um, we didn't see you in our classroom…" Raj said.

"Nor you." Preetha added.

"We got put into another section!" Ryan said.

"Yes! They did!!" Aakriti added.

"We gotta go! See ya later!" Priya said and pushed them forward towards the bus.

They all climbed in and took their seats.

"So, you two to my house?" Aakriti asked.

"Yeah." Priya said.

"You know what's happening in my book?" Aakriti started.

Priya and Devesh sighed inwardly.

Aakriti rambled on about how interesting her book was the entire trip to her house.

"SO!" Devesh interrupted. "Can we do homework when we reach home?"

"SURE!" Priya said

"Uh…ok?" Aakriti said. "And it's not *your* home, it's *mine*!"

"The amount of time we spend there will make everyone think we live there." Devesh muttered.

"What?" Aakriti asked.

"Nothing." Devesh said.

Priya giggled.

Aakriti side-eyed them but she left them alone.

"Um…what is homework?" Alisa asked.

Aakriti took it as her job to explain it to her.

Surprisingly, even Ryan didn't know what it meant.

Halfway through Aakriti's explanation they reached the bus stop.

The five of them emptied out of the bus and walked the rest of the way to her house.

"Hey, Amma!" We're home!" Aakriti yelled.

"Okay sweetie!" Her mom called back from her room.

"Hey, Auntie, we're gonna do our homework." Devesh said.

"Sure." Aishwarya, Aakriti's mom, said as she walked down the stairs.

"Cool. So we're gonna borrow Alexa." Priya said.

"Why?" Aishwarya asked.

"For songs and questions about the homework." Priya replied.

"All right." Aishwarya walked into the kitchen and got started on the preparations for dinner.

"So, what's the real reason you wanted to take Alexa?" Devesh asked Priya.

"Because if Alisa or Ryan had a question they can ask Alexa and we don't need to answer them." Priya said.

"Good idea." Aakriti said.

They all got out their books and settled on the coffee table in the living room.

"So, Alisa and Ryan, if you have any questions on anything you can just say 'Alexa' and ask your question." Priya explained. "Like this, Alexa," Priya waited for the ping. "Wait, why isn't it working?" She wondered, unable to notice that it wasn't plugged in.

Aakriti and Devesh tried their best not to laugh but Devesh let a snicker slip by. "That's because it's not plugged in."

Priya turned bright red with embarrassment. She plugged in Alexa and waited for it to load.

"Alexa," She tried again. This time, it responded immediately. "What day is it today?"

"Today is Tuesday, December 18th." Alexa said

"Alexa, play the song Fearless." Devesh asked.

"Okay. Playing the song Fearless by Lessearfim."

"Please decrease volume by 4 points." Aakriti said.

The volume instantly reduced.

"Cool!"Alisa exclaimed. "Alexa, what are ironans?"

"I'm sorry, I do not know the answer to that question." Alexa said.

"Alexa, resume Fearless." Devesh said.

"Resuming Fearless by Lessearfim." Alexa responded.

"Alexa, what is the meaning of the word 'distilled'?"Alisa asked.

"To make a liquid pure by heating it until it becomes a gas and then cooling it until it is a liquid again : to purify a liquid by distillation." Alexa responded.

"Ok. Could you please repeat?" Alisa asked.

Alexa repeated the definition and Alisa copied it down.

"You can't ask Alexa to do your homework!" Aakriti protested.

"You said that I could ask it any question." Alisa pointed out.

Before Aakriti could retort, a familiar figure strode into the room. He wasn't only familiar to Aakriti, Ryan and Alisa also felt like they saw this man somewhere else as well…

Chapter 8
The Surprising Reunion

Present day, 2 days later, Planet Earth of the Milky Way Galaxy, India, Hyderabad, Kukatpally

"Nanna!" Aakriti exclaimed, Aakriti's father, Sanjiv Kumar, hadn't changed much since she last saw him, the same dark hair and twinkling brown eyes. Aakriti was an exact copy of her father. "I thought you'd come on the twentieth!" Aakriti said.

"Well, I managed to get out earlier." He replied.

"Hi, Sanjiv uncle." Priya said.

Sanjiv grinned. "Good to see my daughter still has her trusty friends at her side."

"Hi, uncle," Ryan said. "We're the new exchange students who'll be staying here…"

Sanjiv smiled uncertainly. "Of course! The more the merrier."

"I feel like I've seen you somewhere." Alisa wondered aloud.

"You do remind me of someone..." Sanjiv said doubtfully.

Aakriti interrupted,"Anyways, what's for dinner?"

"Your favourite!" Auntie said as she came into the room, wearing her lavender coloured apron.

"Pasta?" Aakriti asked, confused.

"No, silly, your Nanna's favourite!" Aakriti's Amma said. "Chicken Biryani!"

"Aw..." Aakriti said.

"You've had pasta for the pasta-two days!" Her Amma said, She waited for someone to point out her pun. "You know, *pasta-two days*?"

"Now we know where Aakriti gets her puns from." Priya muttered.

Devesh snickered. Aakriti shot them both a glare.

Her Nanna laughed, mostly because he forgot how many cheesy puns Aakriti's Amma used to say when he was around more often. "Let's have dinner shall we?"

"Actually, I think I'll skip...my Amma said she'd make Tandoori Paneer for dinner today and well ... :chicken isn't exactly vegetarian." Priya said.

"Well, if Priya's leaving then I'm leaving too." Devesh said which earned him a few odd looks from them. He blushed bright red, " I mean, I don't want to intrude on a family dinner, and since, you know, Priya's also your friend and she's leaving, I thought it was best if this was an 'only family' dinner?"

Aakriti tried not to laugh at his cover-up but one giggle slipped out. Devesh glared at her, she simply shrugged and shot him a look that said 'well, you laughed too, and you didn't even make an attempt to hide it!'

"No problem." Sanjiv said.

Priya and Devesh said goodbye to everyone and walked themselves to the door.

"So, can we start?" Sanjiv said. "I'm starving."

"Oh! Yes, of course" Aishwarya, Aakriti's mom, said. "That flight journey must have been exhausting! Tokyo is really far away."

When Aakriti's parents were out of earshot, Alisa walked over to Aakriti. "What is 'Chicken Biryani?" She whispered.

Wow, Aakriti thought *I think that's the quietest she's ever been!*

As Aakriti observed her face she realised that Alisa looked worried, in fact, she looked *very* worried and so did Ryan

"Hey guys, are you okay?" Aakriti asked them. "This isn't just about the biryani, is it?"

"It can't be him, right?" Alisa blurted out abruptly.

"No, no it-it can't, can it?" Ryan stammered.

"What? Who can't be him?" Aakriti asked.

Auntie poked her head into the living room "Are you guys coming for dinner?" She asked.

"We'll be right there Amma." Aakriti said, waiting for Ryan and Alisa to elaborate but instead they just went through the doorway into the dining room. Aakriti sighed and shook her head but she had nothing to do except follow them.

Aishwarya got the biryani from the stove and almost burned her hands.

Aakriti's Nanna laughed and helped her get the biryani to the table.

They started digging into the food.

There was an awkward silence at first but Sanjiv broke it. "So, how have you been doing these days, Aakriti?"

"Fine, I guess, nothing different since you last left." Aakriti said, though it came out more harshly than she expected it to.

Her father just looked at his plate guiltily and continued eating.

This time Aakriti's mother tried to break the silence. "How was Tokyo?" She asked.

"Good. I managed to make the deal with the company." Sanjiv responded.

"That's nice!" Aishwarya said.

"So Aakriti, what do you want for Christmas this year?" Sanjiv asked.

Before Aakriti could respond, "Ah!" Alisa winced. She sucked her index finger. It looked like she scratched it to the sharp edge of the table.

"Oh, sweetie! Are you okay?" Auntie asked, and she rushed to get the bandages. She tried to get Alisa to show it to her but she kept pulling back. "It's okay, I won't hurt you."

Aakriti watched with anticipation, hoping and hoping that an Ironans blood was red.

Aishwarya yanked Alisa's finger closer to her to get a better look at it. She gasped.

Aakriti got what she wished for.

"What, is it really bad?" Sanjiv said as he came to get a good look at it, what he saw did make him gasp but not because of the reason Aishwarya did.

Alisa's blood wasn't the deep red humans usually had, her blood was the brightest red you'd have ever seen, it hurt to even look at it.

Aakriti winced at the same time Ryan fumbled to come up with an explanation.

Sanjiv looked up slowly. "You're not human, are you? That is definitely the blood of an Ironan."

Chapter 9

THE SECRETS REVEALED

Present day, 2 days later, Planet Earth of the Milky Way Galaxy, India, Hyderabad, Kukatpally

Ayan gasped. "So it is you then."

"I think it's time you all introduce your true selves." Sanjiv said, slowly pulling out a rolling pin from the kitchen counter.

"Sanjiv? What's going on? What the hell is an Ironan?" Auntie asked.

"We don't have time to explain, Amma." Said Aakriti urgently. "Nanna? What does he mean by that? Nanna, please don't tell me you're one of them."

"Aakriti, wait." Sanjiv said firmly as he tapped the rolling pin on the kitchen counter in an intricate pattern. It suddenly retracted into a 3-foot long sword with a glowing blade. Aakriti and the others gasped. "Now you tell me why the General sent you." Sanjiv said.

Alisa whimpered, unable to make any sounds.

Ryan took a deep breath. "We *are* Ironans and we are from Astra but the General didn't send us. We found a portal and jumped through it and as for who we are, I am Ayan Xanner and this is my sister Alera Xanner, our father is Aenan Xanner and our mother is Aurora Raoul."

Sanjiv stared at him for another moment and put his sword down.

"Are you really him?" Alera blurted. "The Exiled One?"

Sanjiv sighed. "Is that what they're calling me these days? "

"You're Astra's number one most wanted criminal." Ayan said. "General Aria won't stop searching for you."

"General Aria? You mean General Auy?" Sanjiv said.

"You really don't know?" Ayan said, "General Aria said you killed General Auy and that you ran away."

"WHAT?" Sanjiv said. "SHE DARES TO FRAME ME A MURDERER?"

CRASH!

A sound erupted from the front yard, Ayan and Alera ran to the window to see what the commotion was.

They gasped.

"Isn't that Aunt Amara's submarine?" Alera said.

"Yes!" Ayan replied. "I never knew it was a spaceship."

Hysterical giggles erupted from Aishawarya's mouth. "This is all some sick joke right? Just to spite me?"

Aakriti looked sad. "No Amma. It isn't."

"But-but can't b-be what they're saying he is…..h-he can't!" Auntie fumbled to say.

"Amma, look, even I don't know i-if Nanna is one of *them* but right now, we don't have time to explain. I think Alera and Ayan's parents have arrived and we have to let them go back to their home. But Nanna and 1 promise that after that we will explain everything." Aakriti said and glanced at her Nanna. He nodded.

Auntie took a shaky breath. "All right."

Alera and Ayan rushed to the front yard, closely followed by the Kumars.

They saw their aunt Amara's ship only inches away from crashing into the house.

The submarine was made of a large hunk of silver-white metal called Rhodium, with the marks of many battles clearly visible on it. Amara Xanner was sort of what humans call a pirate, she sailed or rather *submarined* across Astra's 9 seas, fighting all of Astra's thieves who tried steal cargo ships full of precious metals.

The door slowly opened, and inside was Alera and Ayan's parents, only, they weren't alone.

Arora and Adjin stumbled out of the vehicle, behind them Alera and Ayan's elder brother Ayun, fully dressed in an Astran military uniform. As they looked closer, they realised that Ayun was pointing two guns right at Arora and Adjin's temples. They were gagged with their hands tied behind their backs.

Alera screamed as she saw them emerge. "AYUN! WHAT ARE YOU DOING?!"

Ayan was very pale, he almost looked like he was going to faint.

Behind them, two other figures came into focus and they now understood why their family was cooperating. The two figures were General Aria and Asaya. Asaya was still in her college uniform, her clothes torn to rags. General Aria was holding her by her hair, a knife placed at her throat.

For a moment everyone seemed too shocked to say anything, then suddenly Ayun gave out a cry of anguish. "You promised you wouldn't hurt her!"

General Aria grinned evilly. "I promise many things."

Azul got out his sword. "This seems to be quite the family reunion, don't you think, Aria?"

"Oh, yes." Aria sneered. "Yes, it will be much more fun when all the soldiers behind your house come raging at you, including an angry Arol, who thinks *you* killed our father. Then, it will *truly* be a family reunion. Don't *you* think, Azul?"

Azul snarled and chaos broke out. Azul beelined for Aria, his sword lashing out wildly, not caring if he hit Asaya or not.

Ayun removed the guns from his parents' temples and instead pointed them at the soldiers who were moving from behind the house, swarming the entire place.

Aria parried every stroke Azul threw at her elegantly, all while not losing her grip on Asaya's hair.

The soldiers assaulted Aakriti and her Amma, Aakriti's Amma screamed and pulled Aakriti into the house, away from the fighting.

Chapter 10
THE BATTLE

Present day, 2 days later, Planet Earth of the Milky Way Galaxy, India, Hyderabad, Kukatpally

"Hey, Priya?" Devesh said as they walked away from Aakriti's house. "Um…uh…I.."

Priya raised an eyebrow. "What?"

"Never mind." Devesh muttered.

Suddenly, a loud crash echoed from Aakriti's house and something came crashing down the sky right beside their window..

"Hey, do you think they're in trouble?" Devesh asked.

"Is *that* what you wanted to say?" Priya said.

"Um…no…but *do you think they are in trouble?*" Devesh said.

"Uh, not really, probably just that Aakriti's father accidentally threw the biryani out the window." Priya said, unconcerned.

Suddenly, the sound of clashing swords and bullets echoed behind them.

"Is there any chance that's just the sounds of a really loud action movie?" Devesh asked as they turned back to Aakriti's house.

"Nope…clearly not." Priya said.

Aakriti looked through the window from her house into the horror unfolding in the front yard. She wanted to help them or at least scream but she was frozen in shock as she looked at her father's duel with the General.

"Oh, Aakriti! What do we do?" Her mother said.

"I-I don't know, Amma, I don't know." Aakriti stammered.

She gasped as her father narrowly missed having his head cut off.

Abruptly, her mother shouted in surprise and a loud metal thunk sounded from behind her. Aakriti turned to find an unconscious Astran soldier on the floor behind her and holding an umbrella she plucked from the stand beside the door.

Her mom, Aishwarya laughed nervously and put the umbrella back in the stand.

Suddenly, an idea struck Aakriti. "Hey, Amma, grab two of those umbrellas. We're going to go help."

Aakriti and her mom walked out of the house and went to help the others.

Priya and Devesh popped up at the front gate and walked towards it. As they approached their house, they soon realised that they must try their best to help. Priya dashed into their house, and grabbed two of the most heaviest, damage-inducing utensils she could find.

Devesh looked horrified as the battle before him progressed, whereas Priya, on the other hand, looked thrilled, as if she couldn't wait to smack the Astran soldiers with her cast-iron pan.

Aakriti and her mother, including Priya and Devesh, knocked all of the other soldiers unconscious with their not-so-hostile weapons.

Soon, most of the heavily armed soldiers were passed out on the ground and the rest fled to the portal in the backyard. Only one particularly burly soldier remained, he stayed as close to Aria as possible so Priya assumed he was the General's bodyguard.

Aakriti barely noticed but all the neighbours peeked at this unusual scene from their windows. Few of them screamed or ran away. But many of them just thought they were going crazy and locked the doors to their houses.

Now, the only fight going on was Azul's and Aria's, Asaya seems to have escaped Aria at some point and now stood with her family at the edge of the duel.

It was eerily quiet, no sounds except the clashing of blades.

Aakriti was so intent on watching the battle, just like the others. So she barely noticed when her mother crept up behind Aria, poised with her umbrella to knock her out but, just when she was swinging her umbrella to the General's head, she abruptly turned and her mother ended up hitting Azul right on the head.

Chapter 11
The Trip Through the Portal

Present day, Planet Earth of the Milky Way Galaxy, India, Hyderabad, Kukatpally

"No!" Aakriti said but it was too late. Azul had collapsed to the ground.

General Aria smiled. "Thank you for making this so much easier! Really, that fight was getting so exhausting. Arol, would you please take all of our new prisoners into the ship?"

"Hmm…maybe not. The portal is a much faster way. Take us there!" General Aria addressed the burly soldier.

"Yes, General." Arol saluted, he held Azul's body like a sack of potatoes and threw him into the ship. He slowly approached her Amma and snapped handcuffs on her. "NO!" Aakriti screamed.

"Come on! Do hurry up! We have a public execution to get on with!" Aria said, a wicked smirk on her face and an evil glint in her eyes.

Gasps went around the group.

"You wouldn't!" Ayan and Alera's Amma said.

She was in shock till Arol snapped handcuffs on her hands.

"General?" Arol asked. "Shall I leave the other humans here?"

"No, they know too much. Maybe after we clean their minds. But probably not." Aria said.

She was *so* cruel. Aria would *pay*.

Arol pushed them all into the ship. The pilot, who they later found out was Amara Xanner, started the ship and they flew to the backyard and through the portal.

They zoomed through the green vortex, in a way that Aakriti never thought was possible.

It was as if they were moving faster than the speed of sound, maybe even the speed of light, but she quickly deemed that as highly unlikely.

The ship stopped as soon as it started and as she peeked out of the windshield she saw a sparse desert land with a forest a few yards away.

"Um-" Priya started.

"No talking." Arol told her.

"But-" She tried again.

"Arol, please shut them up." Aria said.

They were pushed out of the ship and onto the desert land.

"Oh don't let them all go!" Aria called, still inside the ship. "I want Azul's child with me!"

Aakriti sucked in a breath and tried to stay calm. What could Aria possibly want to do with her?

Her mother yelped and tried to break free of her bonds.

"She will hold fast?" Aria asked Arol.

"Of course! You think our chains are too weak to be broken by a human?" Arol said.

"Of course not! I just thought she *wasn't* human. I mean, who knew Azul would marry one?" Aria snapped.

Aakriti's mom was about to say something but Arol gagged her mouth with a cloth.

"Now hurry up! I don't have all day!"

Arol rolled his eyes. "Sometimes I can't believe I put up with this family for so long." He muttered.

As Arol dragged Aakriti into the ship, her friends watched helplessly, wishing they could rescue her.

At the last possible moment, Priya did the most stupid thing possible, she jumped into the ship right before it closed.

"Priya!" Aakriti gasped

Priya lost her balance, unable to use her hands to steady herself, she toppled to the floor and groaned in pain.

"What is she doing here?" Aria roared.

"She jumped in." Arol said.

"GET HER OUT!"

"Too late for that!" Arol yelled back over the sound of the starting engine, the ship zoomed into space and out of the atmosphere.

"Arol!" Aria cursed. "How could you let that *human* come in?"

"I really don't like how you keep insulting our species." Priya said as she struggled to get herself up.

"They aren't insults, they're facts. Humans are weak. Pathetic." Aria sneered. "They don't have any idea on how to evolve and advance. Using the same inventions for decades, disgusting."

Priya finally got to her feet."Wait, now you're saying-mmmmhh!" Arol gagged Priya.

"If one word comes out of you, I will do much worse than put a cloth in your mouth." Arol threatened.

Aakriti nodded vigorously.

"Sit down. This is going to be a long ride." Aria let out a wicked laugh.

Priya tried to say "You really need to work on your evil laugh" but it came out more like "Mmm mmm mmmmmmh"

They zoomed through the galaxy. Everytime they passed a beautiful planet, Aakriti crossed her fingers and hoped that it was the planet that they were going to land on but it never was.

They passed breathtaking solar systems and went through asteroid belts. It felt as if days had passed. Finally, they slowed down near a small planet which was in the shape of a crushed tin can.

"What planet is that?" Aakriti asked, curiosity taking over her. Her eyes widened and she clamped a hand over her mouth after she realised that she talked.

Aria didn't seem to notice. "Are you serious?" She reproached. "It's not a planet! It's a moon."

Chapter 12

THE HABITABLE MOON

Present day, Moon No. 97 of Planet Evian, Magellanic Cloud, Near Unnamed Asteroid Belt 21473

"What? How can you live on a moon?" Aakriti asked.

Aria sighed. "I forgot how small-minded humans are. Yes, you can live on moons. This is one of the few moons in this galaxy which is habitable"

"Oh." Aakriti was too shocked to realise the insult Aria added.

Aria rolled her eyes. "Humans." She muttered.

Priya mumbled some very rude words. Luckily, the cloth around her mouth muffled them.

The pilot steered the ship towards the moon and landed it onto the surface.

"Arol, take them out." Aria said.

Arol knocked both Priya and Aakriti on the head. They both collapsed to the ground.

"Why did you do that?" Aria demanded.

"You said take them out."

"Meaning drop them outside!"

"You should be more clear next time."

"Maybe you should be smarter."

Arol's eyes flashed with anger. "Maybe *you* should."

"Excuse me?"

"Nothing, General."

Aria glared at Arol. "Put them outside."

"Isn't that dangerous?"

"Put. Them. Outside."

"Yes, General."

Arol carried Priya and Aakriti outside and set them on the ground. He walked back into the ship and the pilot took off into the atmosphere.

Aakriti groaned as she woke up, her body feeling very sore. She looked around where she was. Momentarily, Aakriti forgot where she was. Then her memories before she was unconscious came back to her, she looked around her surroundings.

It seemed to be like a cave. She found that Priya was still unconscious beside her.

"Hello?" She yelled. "Is anyone here?"

"Wow, humans are even dumber than I expected." A boy's voice came from deeper inside the tunnel. "What would have happened if it was a monster instead of me? You and your friend there would have been eaten."

Aakriti looked all around the cave. "Who are you?"

The voice sighed. "Nope, even dumber."

Priya mumbled something and propped herself up on her elbows. "What happened?" She asked Aakriti.

"Come on." The voice said again.

"Who's that?" Priya asked, much more alarmed.

A laugh echoed around the cave. "I won't hurt you. If I wanted to, you two would be dead already."

"It's really hard to believe that when we can't see you." Priya pointed out.

"Alright." The voice said, and suddenly an african-american boy wearing a leather jacket and jeans came into view.

I wonder how he found those on a moon

Aakriti thought.

Priya snorted. "You don't look so impressive."

The boy took out two huge ray-guns from an invisible pocket. "Is this better?"

"It's definitely much cooler." Aakriti remarked.

"Let's just go." The boy said.

"Go where?" Priya asked.

"You'll see."

"Why should we trust you?" Priya said

"Well, there's no food or water here and with the amount of oxygen inside you're gonna die in about twenty-two hours. If you're humans and not some secret aliens in disguise."

Aakriti and Priya shared a look. "Ok. But you have to help us get a way out of here."

The boy almost laughed at that. "You're serious? Well, I'll see what we can do."

"We?" Aakriti asked.

The boy ignored her and walked deeper into the cave with Aakriti and Priya behind him.

"Hey, you really didn't introduce yourself." Priya said as they were walking into the extensive rocky hallway.

"Hmm, and you did?" The boy said.

"Fine. My name is Priya and my friend's name is Aakriti. We're both from Earth. Happy?"

He sighed, " My name is Agnar."

Priya stifled a giggle.

Agnar glared at her.

"Sorry." She apologised

"So what species are you?" Aakriti asked.

Agnar ignored her again. "Here, we're there."

The tunnel ended at a yawning doorway with a pitch black-room beside it.

"Uh…are you sure that's safe?" Priya asked.

Aakriti walked closer to it and peered inside.

Agnar rolled his eyes and pushed Aakriti into the doorway.

Aakriti yelped and suddenly let out a gasp of surprise. "Priya, you've got to come in here!"

"Is that enough proof for you?" Agnar rolled his eyes.

Priya glared at him but went through the doorway and what she saw almost made her faint.

The room stretched out, its walls and floor crafted from a marble that glowed softly, casting an ethereal light that made the space feel both vast and otherworldly.

"Welcome!" A man's voice said from the other side of the clearing. "To the Garden of Life."

Chapter 13
THE GARDEN OF LIFE

Present day,

Refugee Organisation of the Universe, Moon No. 97 of Planet Evian, Magellanic Cloud.

"That's a very cliche name. I mean, you could have tried a little harder." Priya pointed out.

The man sighed. "I know, I get that a lot." He had curly black hair and was wearing a shining white cloak.

"Oh, come on, Aleph, change back into your true form." Agnar chided. "And this place is NOT the garden of life."

"Aww…you take the fun out of everything!" Aleph said but obediently changed into her true form, which was apparently a dark-haired girl with purple eyes who was wearing the same leather jacket and clothes as Agnar. "Oooh! New recruits?"

"What does she mean by 'new recruits'?" Aakriti asked.

"You'll see." Agnar said.

"You've really gotta stop saying that." Priya said.

"Whatever." Agnar said.

He led them into the main corridor that branched off from the room we were in.

They followed him into the hallway and past many doors, some filled with kids Aakriti's age and others locked with thick metal chains.

Finally, they reached a door with a desk and a boy with scales instead of hair sitting behind it, he was scrolling through a holographic screen in front of him.

"Vin'nyla, Could you please create two profiles for our new refugees?" Agnar requested him.

Vin'nyla nodded and started working on the holographic screen. He gestured for them to move towards the hologram and took a few snaps on the screen.

Agnar led them towards the corridor in the room. "These are the dorms, you'll both have to share a room."

"Okay but um…what is this place?" Aakriti asked.

"It's the Refugee Organisation of the Universe." Agnar said.

Priya had to stop herself from laughing. "Of the universe?"

"Well, yes, many species from all over the universe get stranded here…originally this moon was the slave market for the royalty of the universe." Agnar explained.

"But some of us decided to rebel against it and started this organisation…till now we haven't been found out and we don't intend to until this moon becomes inhabitable."

"Wait, can moons become inhabitable?" Priya asked.

"Wow, humans are so small-minded. If a moon can be habitable, then why can't it become inhabitable?" Agnar said.

"Oi, just because our species isn't as advanced as yours, stop calling us small-minded." Priya said angrily.

Agnar chuckled, but his laugh was quite unnerving, reminding Priya and Aakriti of an old witch's cackle "All right … .but humans from Earth, at least, are very dumb."

Without waiting for Priya to retort, he led them to their room. "So this is where you both will be staying… if you want separate rooms, don't bother us, we need rooms for all the refugees to stay in. "

"Also this place isn't like one of your mediocre Earth hotels, so don't ask for 'room service' or anything." Agnar added.

Agnar opened the door of the room they'd be staying in. Aakriti gasped at how big it was. It was made with the same white marble as the entrance hall, with two huge beds on either side of the room and curtains separating them, on each of their beds were the same clothes Agnar and Aleph were wearing. There was a huge dresser near each of the beds, along with two doors leading to separate restrooms. The room had a huge window in between the beds looking out onto the garden outside.

"Wait, is that the Garden of Life?" Priya asked as she went to look out the window.

Agnar groaned. "No! Every time a new refugee shows up Aleph makes them think it's the 'Garden of Life', I should really tell her to stop!"

"Aw…I actually thought that was cool!" Aakriti said.

"Oh well, sorry to disappoint." Agnar rolled his eyes.

"So um do we have any meal times here cause' I'm getting pretty hungry…" Priya said.

"Oh and is the food here vegetarian?" Aakriti asked.

"There's a poster in the common room explaining everything about this place, and yes the food here is vegetarian, only humans can manage to eat cruelly killed animals without feeling guilty." Agnar said. "Right, I have to go now, see you guys at dinner." He excused himself from the room and closed the door.

"So. . . you have any idea where the common room is?" Priya asked.

Aakriti sighed. "Nope."

Aakriti then went through her dresser and started sniffing vigorously.

"Um…searching for somethin'?" Priya asked.

"You don't really believe that Agnar guy right?" Aakriti asked while searching everywhere around the room.

"Why? You don't trust him?"

"Obviously not! What kind of refugee organisation has rooms as luxurious as a palace?"

"Well, I guess that's a bit fishy…" Priya agreed, "But, this place is our only chance to survive."

Aakriti sighed. "I guess you're right."

"Let's go change and search for the common room." Priya said.

"All right."

They both entered their restrooms to change.

Chapter 14
THE HOLE IN THE SKY

Present day, Planet Earth of the Milky Way Galaxy, India, Hyderabad, Kukatpally

All Devesh could do was stare as the spaceship took off into the sky and vanished in a flash of bright light. Devesh walked over to the backyard, hoping the portal was still there.

It was.

YES! Devesh thought. *I can finally be a part of a supernatural adventure! I've dreamt about this for so long.*

Devesh went back to the front of the house. He entered Aakriti's room and peeked out the window. After bracing himself, he jumped off the edge of the windowsill and prayed the portal would suck him in.

His prayers were answered.

Chapter 15
The General of the Astran Army

Present day, Planet Astra of the Olinian Galaxy, 20,345 million light years away from Earth, General Aria's base

"I think I can hear them arguing…" Alera said with her ear pressed to the wall.

"Alera, they're in a different building, I doubt you can actually hear them." Ayan pointed out.

Alera, Ayan and their sister Asaya were stuck in a cell in General Aria's base. The cell was shaped like a tiny circle, it had blue electric bars blocking them from escaping.

"Asaya, do you know where Mom and Dad are?" Alera asked.

Asaya didn't respond. Their sister was disconsolate. Alera tried hard to cheer her up but failed.

Ayan said, "We have to do something! We can't just sit here waiting to be rescued or let out!"

"We *are* doing something!" Alera argued. "We're trying to eavesdrop on Aria and The Exiled One!"

"For the last time, they're not on this block!"

Ayan yelled, losing his patience

Why is my sister so stupid?! He thought.

Asaya finally spoke, "As the oldest sibling, I did not raise you guys right." She sighed.

"Isn't Ayun the oldest?" Alera pointed out.

"No one cares," Ayan yelled again. "We need to get out!"

"Calm down!" Asaya said.

"Now, what do we do? Any ideas?" Alera asked.

Ayan tried touching the blue bars but ended up getting stung.

"Do you have any ideas on what we should do, Asaya?" Alera asked.

"Maybe..." Asaya replied.

"So you married a human, huh?" Aria said to Azul. "Surprising indeed! Who would have thought?" Aria cackled."The great Azul, betrothed to a simple-minded human!"

"And who would have thought, the great General, who is too scared to fight a weak person like me?" Azul snapped back. He slowly started to advance towards the centre of the room, where Aria stood. Very careful with his movements, Azul wasn't discovered by her.

"I never said you were weak, Azul…heck, you're probably the strongest Ironan alive." Aria said. " You can't trick me that easily, my ego isn't as large as you think it is."

"You seemed to have changed since the last time I saw you."

Aria laughed. "So have you, Azul."

"Really?" He raised an eyebrow.

Finally, he waited until he was close enough to Aria and revealed a contraption that was inside his pocket. It was a gun with unusual carvings and a blue glow coming out of its barrel.

"One of my favourite inventions," Azul smirked as he fired it at her. "A stun gun"

"I don't think this will work…" Alera said.

"Shut up, idiot! Try to be positive for once." Ayan snapped back.

"Looks like you're not in a good mood." Alera grumbled.

Obviously I'm not! Can't she understand our situation? Ayan thought

"Stop it, both of you." Asaya said. "I'm trying to focus here.

Asaya somehow managed to find the keypad in the wall, which could open their cell. She used her hairpin to unscrew the covering and started to play around with the wires inside it.

Finally, Asaya connected a blue wire to a shining yellow one.

The blue electric bars disappeared and we walked out into the plain white hallway.

"Where do we go?" Alera asked.

"How the hell would I know?" Ayan yelled.

Everyone is seriously getting on my nerves!

"Again, shut up both of you." Asaya rolled her eyes. "We can just walk around till we find an exit." She said,

"Yeah, I guess…" Alera said.

As the stun bullet hit Aria's head, "Where did you get that? Azul?" She stuttered out before she fell to the floor unconscious.

Azul slowly walked towards her slumped figure on the floor and secured handcuffs on her.

Then, he called Arol into the room in my best imitation of Aria's voice.

He walked in and was shocked to see Aria bound on the floor.

Azul smiled at Arol. "You know who the general is now, right?"

He bowed down. "At your service, General."

"Good. Send a troop to the Portal or whatever you call it. We don't know how many humans will walk through."

"But General-"

"Arol, go do what I say or do you want me to force you?"

"No, General."

Chapter 16
The Barren Land

Present day, Planet Astra of the Olinian Galaxy, 20,345 million light years away from Earth, The Portal

Devesh screamed as he was thrown across the portal. It was as if someone was forcing him through it.

Finally, it stopped and he was spit out onto a piece of completely plain desert-like land. He glanced around, it was blissfully empty.

Unusually, there was no vegetation or animals anywhere. Nothing except barren land.

Is this a desert or something? Devesh thought

The entire place had an eerie atmosphere. It heightened his suspicions towards the supposedly alien planet.

He pushed himself off the floor and observed the surroundings. There was an extremely tall barbed wire fence around the area.

He remembers Alera and Ayan telling him that they jumped over it.

They're aliens for sure! He thought. *No average human kid-sorry, no human could ever jump over a fence like that!*

Suddenly, he saw a huge force of blue-uniformed guards marching towards him.

Who the hell are they?

Chapter 17
THE ESCAPE

Present day, Planet Astra of the Olinian Galaxy, 20,345 million light years away from Earth, General Aria's base

After walking around the prison aimlessly for who knows how long, Alera's legs were starting to hurt.

"How much longer?" She whined.

"HOW THE HECK WOULD I KNOW?" Ayan screamed.

"Calm down! Both of you are starting to get on my nerves!" Asaya yelled.

I sighed.

"Wait, I think I found a way out…" Ayan said, pointing to a window on my right. It was sealed with a number lock. "Alera, If you climb up on my shoulders, we might be able to get out!"

She sighed again, annoyed. "Fine."

She began to slowly climb on to Ayan's shoulders and peeked out the window. No one was around.

"What code should I try first?" She asked.

"How about the General's birthday?" Asaya suggested.

"Nah, try 1021." Ayan said.

"Why that number?" Alera asked.

"It's the number of cells in the whole compound." Ayan said

"1-0-2-1" She said as she typed in the numbers.

Suddenly, the lock opened.

"Oh my lord of Astra!" Alera exclaimed. "It was right!"

"Yes!" Ayan pumped his fist.

She opened the window and climbed on to the windowsill. The drop was 2 floors high. She felt the wind on her face as she looked downwards. She was never truly afraid of heights.

She jumped.

The wind around her seemed cold and comforting, like the blow of an air conditioner in the hot summer months. She dropped to the ground. The grass cushioning her fall.

Once again, Ayan fell on top of her, screaming.

"Ugh," Alera groaned. "Get off me!"

Asaya fell down next to us gracefully. She got up and pulled Ayan off me. Ayan and Alera stood up and stretched.

"Seriously, if you do this again-"

"Ok, ok. I swear I won't." Ayan said.

"This happened before?" Asaya sighed. "You guys are stupider than I thought."

"Actually, it happened twice before." Alera pointed out. "And it was always Ayan's fault!"

"My fault?!"Ayan exclaimed "It wasn't my fault that you decided to stay there when you knew I was going to jump!"

"Since when did you guys fight so much?" Asaya rolled her eyes.

Ha! As if she was there for half our lives anyways. Ayan thought, *She probably doesn't even remember how old we are.*

"Let's just go," Alera said.

They slowly made their way around the base.

"Well, well, well....Look what we have here!" A voice boomed from behind them. "I genuinely thought you guys wouldn't be able to break out."

Chapter 18
THE DINING HALL

Present day,

Refugee Organisation of the Universe, Moon No. 97 of Planet Evian, Magellanic Cloud.

Aakriti and Priya finally figured out where the common room was, after at least an hour of searching. The huge holographic poster in the centre of the room explained the rules, mealtimes and details of the place.

It was surrounded by comfy couches and armchairs. The circular room's walls were lined with books from top to bottom.

"Is the time system different here or somethin'? Why does the poster say dinner time at the 24th ring?" Priya wondered aloud.

"Hm…probably is. Maybe the 'ring' refers to the ring of a bell." Aakriti speculated.

"You sure about that?" Priya raised her eyebrows.

Aakriti sighed. "Honestly, I'm not sure about anything anymore."

"Hey-" Priya started only to be interrupted by the abrupt gong of a bell.

Slowly, all the people, or rather, aliens, started to pour out of the common room, in an almost robotic manner, into an adjoining doorway.

Priya and Aakriti had no choice but to follow as they were pushed in with the flow of the crowd.

The dining hall was just as grand as the entrance hall.

Priya gazed in awe at the rich brown tables draped with pale silk cloth, and even more at the platters of colourful dishes that were set over it. "It looks like it's straight from a Harry Potter movie." She exclaimed.

Aakriti wasn't able to share Priya's admiration for the place and was instead sceptical of the beauty of the hall. She continued to wonder how a refugee organisation managed to be this luxurious.

As far as she knew, refugees were people who barely managed to escape death and had little to nothing with them, but it looks like the universe had a different idea of 'refugees'.

Aakriti continued to stare in suspicion of everything around her.

Priya pulled her hand and dragged her towards the centre table. Agnar was waving them over.

She followed Priya, still knowing that something was definitely off about this place.

Chapter 19
The Blue-Uniformed Soldiers

Present day, Planet Astra of the Olinian Galaxy, 20,345 million light years away from Earth, The Portal

Devesh continued to stare at the blue-uniformed soldiers who marched towards him rapidly, and in an unusually synchronised manner. He thought it better for him to hide rather than face them so he quickly ran towards the forest near the right of the land. He made it inside and quickly ducked under a bush from which he could get a clear view of the moving soldiers.

They reached the chasm and broke their ranks to search the perimeter.

One of the soldiers said, "I could swear I saw a person standing here.."

"I really doubt we can trust your eyes, you have really poor vision, Lieutenant Asan."

Lieutenant Asan sighed. "That is true. My sight continues to deteriorate as I age."

"Stop chatting and start searching!" Another soldier barked.

"Yes, sir!" The other two replied.

Devesh continued to watch their search and listened to their conversations. He managed to slowly capture snippets of information, he heard them talk of Aria and how Azul knocked her down so quickly, the soldiers were happy Aria was gone as they believed she was some sort of a dictator. He also heard them talk of humans and how they are pests and that the need for them to close the portal was extremely dire.

Since he was so focused on listening to what the other soldiers were saying, he didn't even feel it when Lieutenant Asan shot him in the back with a stun gun.

Chapter 20
THE EXILED ONE

Present day, Planet Astra of the Olinian Galaxy, 20,345 million light years away from Earth, General Aria's base

Alera, Ayan and Asaya swivelled their heads in the direction of the noise. Their jaws dropped to see the Exiled One with the General's cap and badge.

"Honestly though, I never thought you guys had it in you." The Exiled One continued.

Alera gazed in total disbelief and finally stuttered out, "Are you the General now?"

"But it can't be! How can The Exiled One be allowed to become the General?" Asaya asked.

"Technically, it's possible." Ayan replied. "It's in the Rules and Laws of Astra, page 128, 'Any citizen brave enough to challenge the General, can be granted the title if they win. This counts for not only currently residing citizens, but exiles as well.'"

"Wow! You seem to be very well-versed in the Laws of Astra. You must also be aware that breaking out of the Astran prison's penalty is death." Azul replied. "And honestly, you kids should stop calling me 'The Exiled One'. I'm the General now and I expect to be referred to as General Azul."

Ayan smiled triumphantly ."Yes, General Azul, but you fail to mention a key point which is written in the Astran constitution, 'No child below the age of 15 can be arrested and/or put under house arrest.'"

Azul raised an eyebrow. "I expected that rule to change after I'd heard of Aria's ascendance. Surprising, considering the fact that she was a tyrannical ruler…"

"That was one of the few unchanged laws from when our father was the general, Azul." A new voice piped in.

Azul smiled with familiarity in the direction of the voice.

Slowly, a figure creeped out of the other side of the compound.

"I was wondering when you'd show up to take your rightful place as the general." Anel smirked

"And I was wondering when you would try to overthrow your beloved sister, but it seems like that never happened." Azul retorted.

"Who is that?" Alera whispered to Ayan.

Ayan curses."How the hell would I know?" He muttered back. "Well, since you spend your whole day poring over books of Astran history, I was betting you would know something about the General's family." Asaya joined in. *Well, maybe she does know something about us after all.* Ayan thought.

"You kids can stop your murmurs now. It's not as if it would make a difference, I can hear all of you as clear as day." Azul said as he observed their supposedly 'secret' exchange of words.

"Your hearing seems to be as sharp as ever." Yet another unfamiliar voice added. This one was as shrill as it was accented and distinctly seemed to be that of a girl's.

"I thought living with the humans for so long would blunt the sharp knife you are. But I believe I was proven wrong." An elegant woman strode into the figure, her eyes smouldering and filled with defiance, just like Aria's.

Azul's playful manner dissipated. He stared at the woman, astonished. "I never thought I'd see you again, Aya."

Chapter 21
The Traitorous Ally

Present day,

Refugee Organisation of the Universe, Moon No. 97 of Planet Evian, Magellanic Cloud.

Priya and Aakriti waded through the swarm of people and finally made their way to Agnar. The smell of the food seemed to be intoxicating. In fact, the food looked too good to be true. A cheese-filled puff of some kind was paired with a burnt-garlic sauce and surprisingly, many of the dishes smelled and looked similar to the dishes from Italy.

Agnar aggressively spooned and served all kinds of delicacies onto their wheel-sized plates.

Blinded by their hunger and bewitched by the sickly sweet scent of the food, Priya started to shove food into her mouth as quickly as she possibly could. She was so focused on her food, and how utterly delectable it was, to notice Agnar's wicked smile as she ate.

Aakriti, however, took notice of it. But even she was not strong enough to battle against the hunger pangs that constantly attacked her stomach. Soon, she had no choice but to give in.

Agnar laughed to himself. *Humans and their stupid weaknesses.* He thought. *They almost tempt you to use them as prey.*

After filling themselves to the brim, Aakriti and Priya slowly wobbled out of the enormous dining hall. The bell's gong resounded from the great walls of the room.

The sound seemed to echo in their heads as they struggled to push their feet forward.

Their eyelids started to grow heavy, so heavy, it almost felt as if the weight of the world was pressing on their eyes, beckoning them to close, for them to fall.

The last thing they heard as they both tumbled to the dining hall's pristine marble floor was Agnar's incessant cackling. "I feel like I've won the lottery!" He screeched with glee.

Chapter 22
More Secrets Revealed (Honestly, people have too many secrets)

Present day, Planet Astra of the Olinian Galaxy, 20,345 million light years away from Earth, General Azul's base

"Mother!" Aria shouted as she ran towards the woman.

Ayan and Asaya were right behind her.

She hugged them back, and they stayed that way for a few seconds until Azul said, "You have children?"

Aya smiled at him.. "A lot has changed since you ran away, Azul." In fact, her voice was cold despite her warm smile.

"Mother, you knew the Exiled One?" Alera asked.

"More importantly," Ayan turned towards Azul. "Why did you call my mother Aya?"

"Exactly what I was wondering." Asaya added. "Her name is Aurora Raoul, not Aya."

"What?" Azul paled. "You changed your name? But why.." He trailed off.

"Because of me." Anel said.

"What?" They all said in unison, except Aya.

Anel sighed at the same time Aya let out a deep breath,

"That's a really long story." He sighed again.

"Wait," Aria reeled towards her mother. "You lied to us about your name? You changed it? Does father-"

"How could you?" Ayan interrupted. "Why would you?"

Asaya stared at the same spot on the ground, as if she was deeply concentrating on something. "Wait, I think I know-"

She was cut off by the rumbling of loud footsteps on the ground. The earth was shaking, almost as if an earthquake was coming.

The Astran army came into view and stopped marching in unison. They all bowed to Azul in perfect sync. A man with quite a few badges on his blue button-up coat brought forward a scrawny dark-haired boy who seemed to be slowly regaining his consciousness.

He stared at the scenery around him in utter disbelief. "Wait, plants here are blue?" He slurred before he fell into the dreamless oblivion of unconsciousness once again.

Chapter 23
The Annoyed General

Present day, Planet Astra of the Olinian Galaxy, 20,345 million light years away from Earth, General Azul's base

Just as Asaya was about to voice what she realised, Azul said, "It is not the correct time or place for revelations such as these."

"Well then what would be the correct time and place, our respected General?" Ayan fumed. "Would you care to *enlighten* us?"

Aya put a hand on his shoulder. "He's right, son. You must calm down."

Ayan's jaw twitched with annoyance as he reluctantly obeyed his mother's wishes.

"Well then, since we all seem to be on the same page-"

"Who said we're on the same page?" Alera interrupted.

Azul sighed. "Like I said once, and I will say again, this is *not* the correct time or place for misplaced anger-"

"What do you mean 'misplaced'?" Alera cut in once again. "What, do you think of yourself as some high and mighty-"

He finally lost his composure. "NOW IS NOT THE TIME! DON'T YOU CARE ABOUT YOUR DEAR FRIENDS?" Azul shouted. DON'T YOU CARE ABOUT RESCUING THEM?"

Alera went silent. Embarrassment burned her cheeks as she finally realised she forgot about her friends and was distracted by trivial and selfish matters.

Asaya sighed. "So, what's the plan now?"

"I...'m still figuring that part out," Azul stuttered.

"May I suggest something?" Anel asked.

Alera laughed. "You don't even know where they are or how they were captured."

"Well, whenever Aria captures anyone, she usually puts them in her prison, and if they're not here, there's only one other place they can be." Anel explained.

"Where is that?" Asaya asked.

"The slave moon." Anel said simply.

Ayan exclaims with recognition. "So, that's where she dropped them...I'd wondered if it was that."

"Where is this slave moon?" Asaya asked.

Before Ayan could answer, the slumped figure of the human boy let out a groan.

Chapter 24
THE CATASTROPHIC CONFUSION

Present day, Planet Astra of the Olinian Galaxy, 20,345 million light years away from Earth, General Azul's base

This was by far the weirdest place Devesh had ever woken up in. I mean, he was used to waking up in different places than where he actually slept but this was a whole new level of unusual. This time, he didn't even remember where slept, or when he slept, or, in fact, who he was. Was his name *actually* Devesh?

Was this even real?

His eyes blinked open to take in a horribly unusual scenery, which only added to his skyrocketing feelings of confusion.

First of all, as far as he knew, most plants were *green.* But as he found himself surrounded by a blue sea of foliage, he questioned his knowledge about every trivial matter. Wait, knowledge? What knowledge did he have when he could remember absolutely nothing?

Not only was the greenery in shades of blue, the sun wasn't white either! Wait, isn't the sun yellow?

On top of that, everyone around him seemed to have unusually reddish skin.

Is this what everything is supposed to be like? His addled brain wondered. But, deep down, he knew something was wrong. A feeling of inadequacy grew in the pit of his stomach, as if his body was trying to tell him he didn't belong here.

Something else seemed to be off too. He could hear nothing. His ears, along with most of his other senses (luckily not sight), seemed to have gone numb.

He gazed around at the people nearby, who seemed to be mouthing words extremely aggressively at him.

He tried to push himself up to stand, but his legs weren't cooperating.

Unable to do anything else, he laid there on the unusually soft grassy ground and stared up at the blue plants, intrigued by how much they varied in shade.

Chapter 25

The Surprising Reunion Pt. 2 (this one was not as happy)

Present day, Planet Astra of the Olinian Galaxy, 20,345 million light years away from Earth, General Azul's base

"What's wrong with him?" Alera voiced the thought everyone seemed to be having.

The soldier who brought him cleared his throat, Lieutenant Asan "Well, you see, I thought this boy was a threat, so I *may have* shot him with a stun gun-"

"A stun gun?" Azul asked. "Haven't you been taught that those guns show extremely adverse effects on other species?"

Anel nodded in agreement. "Yes, indeed. They were made by my team and I to be used only on Astrans, that too, in extreme emergencies."

"But, General Aria-" The lieutenant started.

"There is no 'General Aria'." Azul said icily.

"You seem extremely sure of that." A horribly familiar voice interrupted.

Everyone gazed in horror as Aria limped towards them. "You really didn't think you'd get rid of me that easily, Did you?"

Aria's entrance would have been perfectly dramatic, like that scene in movies when the soundtrack reached to its end with a final flourish. But, the climatic air was ruined by the thud of dull metal. Azul thumped Aria on the head with the back of his sword, and slowly eased the weapon back into its scabbard.

"Now, we don't have the time to argue." Azul said, "Time is of the essence. We have no choice but to act now."

This time, no one raised their voice against him.

Everyone solemnly nodded.

Asaya cleared her throat. "Sorry to ruin the…vibe and all, but..um, what are we going to do with them?" She gestured towards the slumped figures of Devesh and Aria on the floor.

Azul then ordered Lieutenant Asan to throw Aria into the deepest cell in the compound. The Lieutenant saluted and did as he was told.

Anel, in response to Asaya's question regarding Devesh, said "I will take him to the medical wing."

"Are you sure that's a good idea?" Ayan piped in. "Considering the fact that Astran medicine wasn't intended-"

Anel cut him off. "I appreciate your concern, but I will merely ensure he isn't in a fatal condition and will expose him only to mild Astran medicine that shows limited side effects."

Asaya clapped her hands. "Alright. Now that that's cleared, I think it's time we go kick some alien butt."

Alera laughed just as Ayan frowned, but they both said in unison, "You sound like a human."

Chapter 26
MEMORIES GO MISSING

Present day,

Refugee Organisation of the Universe, Moon No. 97 of Planet Evian, Magellanic Cloud.

Aakriti blinked, momentarily blinded by a flash of unusually bright orange light. Priya was next to her, seemingly just as disoriented. She shielded her eyes with her hands and as they adjusted, got up to examine her surroundings.

They were in a desolate grey room. It was circular in shape. Its circumference was lit with a strange orange glow, eerily illuminating the prison-like compartment.

She tried to move towards the light, enthralled. Just as she put her foot forward, she was jerked backward and her head hit the ground.

She got up and examined her surroundings yet again. She stared at the gleaming orange circumference as if staring at it for the first time.

I feel like I'm forgetting something... Aakriti thought.

Her brain was addled and she seemed completely unaware of the chain that jerked her backwards just a few moments ago.

She fell back down and her head hit the smooth, nearly opalescent white floor once again.

Aakriti got up, and the vicious cycle seemed to repeat.

Finally, on her fifth try, she supported herself and prevented her head from banging against the floor.

Abruptly, the memories of her previous experiences flooded back into her mind. She clutched her head, which was throbbing like a pulse.

After the pain subsided, she came to her senses and searched for Priya. Unusually, she wasn't there.

Aakriti racked her brain. *How can that be?*

She thought. *Priya was right here until a few seconds ago...*

Suddenly, a familiar malicious cackle resonated through the compartment. The circular room started to gleam, as if all the walls were covered with opals laced with moonlight.

Aakriti's gaze darted around in alarm. *The floor wasn't this bright before, was it?*

The sound grew louder as the compartment heated up until the soles of her feet were almost burning.

Funny. She thought *How come I never noticed I was barefoot before? How come I wasn't able to notice so many things?*

Chapter 27
THE RESCUE MISSION

Present day, Planet Astra of the Olinian Galaxy, 20,345 million light years away from Earth, General Azul's base

"Honestly," Asaya tucked a small dagger into a holster that was attached to the new Astran military uniforms they all donned. "Aren't these weapons way too small?"

"Yeah." agreed Ayan. "How are we going to fight galactic royalty with these?"

"Wait, we're going to fight royalty?"Alera asked, confused

"Yes.." Azul replied. "A slave moon is where they purchase their slaves. If we aren't too late, we can rescue them."

"And if we are?"asked Ayan

"Then they will be lost forever." Azul said curtly.

"And, about the weapons being too small," Aya added. "Press the hilt of any of the knives or daggers."

Ayan and Asaya followed her instructions.

As soon as Asaya put pressure on the hilt, the dagger transformed into a three-foot long sword with a gleaming silver blade and ruby-red hilt.

"Whoa!" She whispered.

Asaya balanced the weapon in both her hands,"Hold on, why is it so lightweight?"

"I think it's made with the rare metal found in-" Ayan started, weighing his own sapphire-hilted version of the blade, before he was interrupted by Azul.

"That is not important right now." He said sternly, "We must travel to the slave moon."

"And how do you suggest we're going to do that?", snapped Ayan bitterly, still annoyed at Azul's intrusion.

Azul's lips curved into a grim smile, "You'll see."

Chapter 28
The Trip Through the Weirder Portal

Present day, Planet Astra of the Olinian Galaxy, 20,345 million light years away from Earth, General Azul's base

Azul took them to the desolate plain of land where the chasm was and dug a hole into the sandy soil. He shot the hole with a gun he had with him. It was an unusual contraption, a hunk of metal engraved with carvings of the Ancient Astran alphabet. This time, the chasm glowed a bright shade of blue, the jarring tint of a blue flame.

Then, as usual, Alera offered to go first, eager to experience the new portal and she very quickly regretted that decision, since Ayan came tumbling behind her.

"I did *not* think there could be an even crazier travel experience after the-" Alera's words were cut off as she screamed, careening through the bright blue vortex.

Ayan joined her, and both of them screamed all the way down.

Alera fell out and finally, she rolled out of the way so Ayan didn't fall over her.

"I think we're getting used to this! You didn't crush me this time." Alera beamed.

Ayan glared at her. "You act like that's a good thing."

Just as she was about to retort, Azul dropped out of the portal and landed gracefully on his feet. Following him, came Asaya and Aya, who both copied his movement perfectly and did not so much as stumble as they toppled out of the electric blue portal.

Alera gazed in shock. *Are we the only Astrans with bad balance?* She thought

She shook her head and exited her thoughts. She slowly took in the whole landscape. *It's really barren...* She thought.

At the same time, Ayan, almost as if he heard her, said. "It really is barren."

The rocky terrain consisted of nothing but caverns and humongous grey boulders for miles on end.

Asaya stared at the jagged landforms. "How do people even survive here?" She wondered aloud.

"They don't." replied Aya, her face a mask of stone.

Chapter 29

The Actual Rescue Mission

Ayan descended down the rocky slope they stood atop. He carefully made his way down, peering into the caves and holes dotted throughout the hill.

Alera ran behind him, and her boot caught on to one of the ragged protruding rocks. She tripped, crashing into Ayan and sending them both careening down into one of the caverns.

She got up and dusted her clothes. Just as she was about to apologise to Ayan for being so careless, a bright orange light, almost like the Earth Sun's glow was replicated in the cave, flashed. Alera was disoriented, and she fell to the floor. She was used to getting flustered due to light but this time, it somehow felt worse. It was like she felt her consciousness slipping away, along with her memories and thoughts. All she felt was the light, pulsing through her veins. No, she didn't feel the light, *she was* the light.

Just as the light was about to consume her, she heard a voice. A strangely familiar voice, though she was sure she had never heard it before.

The owner's voice shook her shoulders, crying, "Alera, wake up, wake up!"

She slowly blinked open her eyes, shielding them from the unusual orange glow that the room they were in emitted. Slowly, the memories which were fading started to come back.

"Oh thank god you're okay! I was so worried…" Ayan was saying.

"Where are we?"stuttered Alera.

"I have no idea," admitted Ayan, "But this is the place they're being kept captive."

Alera asked, "How are you so sure of that?"

"Take a look behind you." He sighed.

She swivelled her head backwards and understood what he meant.

Neither of them were sure who said it, but the words, "How the Hell do we get out of here" were definitely uttered.

Chapter 30
THE TRAPPED TRIO

Refugee Organisation of the Universe, Moon No. 97 of Planet Evian, Magellanic Cloud.

Alera and Ayan paced around the narrow white strip, still shook by what they saw. The wide glass panel, which had a projector positioned towards it, displayed what looked like a camera feed of a jail cell compound.

There were at least 300 adjoining cells (Ayan counted), and Priya and Aakriti were held hostage in one of them.

They continued to rack their brains, trying desperately to brainstorm a way out of the prison.

Suddenly, a rattling scream cut off their train of thought.

Alera and Ayan looked towards the phosphorescent white ceiling in alarm. They gazed, disbelieving, as a spot in the wall grew thin and opened up. Asaya came tumbling down and, for the first time, fell flat on her face.

As soon as her head hit the ground, another one of those spells of vermillion light seemed to engulf the room.

Asaya got up, disoriented, but seemingly unaffected by the light.

"Why aren't you half-dead yet?" asked Alera stupidly.

Asaya stared at her, incredulous, "What?"

Ayan sighed. "When she fell down, the light led to her collapsing, so she assumed the same would happen to you."

"Oh." Asaya said. "Where are we? Is this another prison? Cause' honestly I have no idea how to get us out again."

"I don't think we're *inside* the prison. This place seems more like a waiting room." speculated Ayan.

Unexpectedly, the sound of an uproarious laugh resonated through the radiant white walls.

"You couldn't be more wrong about that!" The owner of the voice wheezed in between his guffawing.

Chapter 31
The Stranded Siblings

Refugee Organisation of the Universe, Moon No. 97 of Planet Evian, Magellanic Cloud.

Aya screamed as she saw Asaya, her third child, fall into the crevice in the rock. She ran after her, but a firm grip on her forearm held her back.

She reeled towards Azul. "How could you let them endanger themselves like that? Aren't you aware that-"

"That they're just children?" finished Azul, sighing.

"Well, yes!"

"But we have no choice." He started to explain, "The prison where they hold the slaves in before they are transported to their new homes, has highly complex defence mechanisms. They usually try to fool the more susceptible species by telling them it's a refugee organisation.

If a person who has too many memories tries to break in, when they come into contact with the walls of the prison, find themselves lost in the vast pathways of their own thoughts, impossible to come out."

Realisation dawned on Aya. "So the only ones who can make the trip are the children...this was your plan all along wasn't it?"

Azul sighed. "If I had told everyone, they would have panicked. And you would definitely not have agreed. No parent willingly allows their children to put themselves in danger."

"You would know about that, wouldn't you, Azul?" said Aya bitterly.

Azul blanched. His voice was tense, as taut as a string. "I never meant any harm-"

She laughed. "Of course you didn't, you also probably didn't know that after you left, the truth got out."

It was almost as if Azul grew even paler than before. "What?"

"Everyone shunned *me* as I grew up, for your disappearance." Aya said. "They called me unnamable things, all because you weren't careful enough with who you told."

"I didn't tell anyone."

Aya scoffed. "*Of course*, you didn't, my dear-"

She was cut off by the rocks underneath their feet rumbling, sending them skidding towards the chasm.

Chapter 32
THE FLYING SERPENT

Refugee Organisation of the Universe, Moon No. 97 of Planet Evian, Magellanic Cloud.

Post its unusually cheery laughter, the voice gave them what seemed like a warning, “If you children want to escape this place, I suggest begging at my feet. But, wait, you can’t do that, since you can’t see my feet!” The voice trailed off with yet another cackle, finally shutting up.

Asaya glared at a spot on the wall, internally screaming at the owner of the obnoxious voice.

Ayan continued his nervous pacing, scratching his head all the way. Occasionally, he would mutter something unintelligible, which led to his sisters shooting him a ‘what the hell is wrong with this guy’ look.

At some point, Asaya got fed up. She turned to him, her face a mask of annoyance, words about to form on her lips as a scream cut her off.

Just as Asaya had fallen out of the ceiling minutes before, Aya came tumbling down, followed by Azul.

Yet again, they landed on their feet gracefully.

Azul's expression was unexpectedly taut, in high contrast to his usually serene arrangement of features.

The voice cackled yet again and Alera's hands curled into fists. She started to shake, as if unable to control her pent-up frustration.

Her vision went black, bright spots dancing across, she punched the opalescent white wall. Instead of her knuckles being bruised and bloody, a long, wide crack emerged in between the white stone. It shone with an orange glow. She let out an earth-shattering scream before her body went limp. She dropped to the floor, which was an illuminated orange as well, and the whole room glimmered with the amber light, before every bit of it started to unravel. The walls shimmered as if they were real moonlight and slowly came apart in shining silver threads. The whole structure shuddered and shook, and the sound of crumbling concrete filled the prison. A piece of rubble made its way into the room, landing squarely on Aya's left foot, as if someone directed towards her.

Aya covered her hands with her mouth, muffling a screech of pain. Azul's face seemed to have gotten tenser. Asaya and Ayan clutched each other, and watched with horror as the huge silhouette of a dragon-like creature emerged. It had tusks the size of elephants (yes, not *like* those of elephants but as big as them) and shimmering scales in every shade of orange possible. From tangerine, to coral, to amber, to vermillion, the serpent's scales flickered, his muscles rippling. The dragon's copper snout broke into a smug grin, his scarlet eyes twinkling and sharply-clawed talons clapping together. "Well, that was quite a show, wasn't it?"

Chapter 33
The Imaginary Infirmary

Present day, Planet Astra of the Olinian Galaxy, 20,345 million light years away from Earth, The Infirmary

Devesh woke with a start and found himself in a strikingly familiar place. It was his school's infirmary, and he was laying on his usual bed. As an abnormally clumsy student, Devesh was a frequent visitor of the sick bay, meaning he was well-accustomed to every nook and cranny of the room (but not in the way you probably imagined, he stubbed his toe on nearly every corner of the place). He almost expected the nurse to walk in, and chastise him for napping here during classes, but the person who walked was definitely not his school nurse.

A man, who had features which were uncannily familiar, strode in with a tray of food. He smiled at Devesh, "Finally up, are you?"

"Y-yeah…" stuttered Devesh. "Have I met you before?"

"Not that I know of."

Devesh stared at the man and felt something tickle in his mind. Abruptly, all the memories of the previous events came flooding back, making him feel as if he had gotten hit by a truck. He leaned towards the bed's headboard, his mind a mess of memories, thoughts and untethered feelings.

The man gazed at him thoughtfully. "I think you could use a bit of this." He offered him a glass bottle filled with a bluish liquid.

A newfound feeling of parchedness seemed to envelope his throat. He grabbed the bottle and guzzled the liquid down. It tasted like water, with an unusually tangy aftertaste

He coughed. "Thank you."

"My pleasure."

The water-like drink seemed to clear his mind enough for him to be able to understand who the man reminded him of.

"Are you related to…" Devesh trailed off, he was about to say Aakriti's father, till he realised the Ironans probably had no idea of his child. He racked his brain, trying to recall what Ayan and Alera called him, "The exiled one?"

Chapter 34
YET ANOTHER ESCAPE (BARELY)

Refugee Organisation of the Universe, Moon No. 97 of Planet Evian, Magellanic Cloud.

Azul gaped in shock as he witnessed the appearance of the tawny scaled-serpent.

Aya, Ayan and Asaya were hunched over the slumped figure of Alera, begging her to wake up. Though shock registered as they saw the appearance of the orange snakelike winged animal, their priorities lie elsewhere.

Slowly, his senses came back to him as realisation dawned. This dragon-like creature was not just a winged viper, but a vicious beast, from one of the most wicked species in the universe, the Yuvunans.

The gears in his brain finally started to twist, clicking together in a variety of ways, trying to find a way to escape and save everyone.

His serene expression returned as he pondered answers for their plight.

The serpent let out a resounding cackle as it shrunk into the figure of a six-foot-tall man and transformed back into the dragon. "I doubt you can find a way out of here." The vicious beast said with a smug smile, his eyes droning into Azul's.

Azul's response was as defiant as his stare. "Then, you know nothing about me." A slow, smug smile of his own spread across Azul's face. He finally seemed to have discovered, or rather, *assumed*, what Yuvunan's weakness was.

Chapter 35
THE COLLAPSING CAPSULE

Present day,

Refugee Organisation of the Universe, Moon No. 97 of Planet Evian, Magellanic Cloud.

Priya paced around the white, capsule-like room. Its circular walls glowed, illuminating the place with unusually pale light. An orange glow lined the circumference, filtering through the cracks in the floor.

As far as she knew, she woke up here at least an hour ago, and she had no idea where Aakriti was.

What she learnt until now was the fact that the floor had the power to somehow erase her memories whenever she touched it to her head and that her ankle was seemingly chained to an unseen weight that limited her movement around the already-tiny room.

Priya had been pondering escape routes and plans for god knows how long, sometimes tripping over her own feet and landing facedown on the opalescent floor, resetting her progress once again. Stuck in this impossible cycle, she was sure that very soon she would drive herself mad, if she already *wasn't* insane.

As she struggled with her plans, the orange glow seemed to grow unduly strong. The light engulfed the whole room in a shade of amber.

An earth-shattering sound assaulted her ears, shaking her out of her thoughts.

Suddenly, the walls of the chamber gave out, she would have been crushed by a shining, abalone shell-like rock if not for her astoundingly fast reflexes.

She silently prayed. *I hope Aakriti's okay.*

The wall on her left crumbled like a dry vanilla cake. Having no other way to go, Priya walked through the newly-formed doorway, making her way through bits and pieces of debris from the collapse.

She stepped into an adjoining chamber, and what she saw made her heart stop.

It was a still body, covered with three huge rocks, and the face was too familiar to forget.

"Aakriti!" yelled Priya as she picked her way to her friend's unmoving body.

She hunched over her, shaking her shoulders and crying her name. Then, finally, her common sense came back to her as her nerves and panic slowly subsided. She checked her pulse and heartbeat, which were steady albeit faint.

She prayed once again, her eyes closed and palms together, putting all of her effort into hoping and wishing her friend comes back to consciousness. Honestly, she did not believe it would work, but when she opened her eyes, Aakriti seemed to have revived. She slowly pushed herself up, somehow able to remove the impossible heavy debris, that Priya couldn't even attempt to lift, with ease

A cough hacked her chest and plumes of dust formed cloud-like shapes around them.

"Where are we?" Aakriti asked.

Priya, too overwhelmed with relief, was unable to answer and instead crushed her in a hug. "I thought you'd never wake up!"

Aakriti shot her a look. "What do you mean?"

Before Priya had the chance to reply, echoing laughter filled the area. Its sound brought Priya anger she had never felt before. She vowed to herself that she would never trust strangers ever again, no matter how dire the situation they were in was.

As Priya immersed herself in thoughts of rage and revenge, she was unable to notice the dark silhouettes making their way through the refuse, heading right towards them.

Chapter 36
THE CAPTIVE TURNED CAPTOR

Present day,

Refugee Organisation of the Universe, Moon No. 97 of Planet Evian, Magellanic Cloud.

Azul reeled towards the rest of the group, "Leave." He ordered. "Go find the others, I'll deal with him."

Yet another cackle resounded from the serpent's direction. "And how would you do that?"

Azul just smiled.

"Are you sure you can do this-" said Ayan, voicing the doubts everyone seemed to have.

Azul waved him off, and told them once more to leave.

The rest, having no other option, made their way across the rubble created due to the crumbled wall.

Little did they know, the collapse of one wall managed to lead to nearly all of the walls of the structure tumbling down.

They picked their way through the refuse, walking towards a destination none of the group was aware of.

Ayan had Alera bundled up in his arms, and he led the way. Asaya walked behind him, supporting their limping mother, Aya.

They finally found themselves in a small, collapsed white capsule.

"It's one of the holding cells." said Ayan weakly, adjusting his grip on his sister's unmoving body.

"Do you think the priso-" Just as Asaya was about to finish, something seemed to muffle her words. Ayan observed a flit of movement, too fast for most people to comprehend, and that was the last thing he saw, before the sound of a dull thunk reverberated through his skull, and he collapsed to the floor in a useless heap.

Aya watched with horror, supporting herself against the remnants of the wall, her injured foot threatening to give out. She fixed the incredulous expression onto her face, and slowly, inch by inch, moved her hand towards the edge of her boot, where she had hid a pistol.

Chapter 37
THE VISIONS

Present day, Planet Astra of the Olinian Galaxy, 20,345 million light years away from Earth, The Infirmary

"Yes." The man replied, amused. "If that's what you call Azul."

"Oh." Devesh said. "So that's his name.."

The man did not respond, and instead stared at Devesh with a quizzical expression, as if he was a dysfunctional machine.

Devesh stared back, curious at why the man looked at him in such a way. "What's your name?"

He flashed an amused smile once again. "Are you really not affected?"

"Affected by what?"

This time, his smile was not so amusing as it was malicious. He grabbed Devesh's arm roughly, "By this."

Devesh gasped, it felt as if all the oxygen around him was being sucked out, leaving him with nothing to breathe in. The air he inhaled was near-poisonous, burning his lungs and throat.

The man's smile elongated, along with his face, making him look like a disfigured creepy clown.

Devesh woke up with a start, and he gazed around the room. He was still in his school infirmary, and the same man was still next to him.

But instead of his face elongated in a frightening grin, his features seemed to be arranged into an expression that could be described as concerned.

Devesh scooted away from the man, the memory of his nightmare too fresh.

"I seemed to have forgotten the side effects of this medicine." The man said, swirling the bottle of blue liquid Devesh had downed.

"Oh." He said. "What are the side effects, exactly?"

"Hm...I believe it leads to excessively vivid dreams, but for Ironans the dreams are usually positive..."

"Mine was anything but that." Devesh snorted.

The man asked thoughtfully, "May I know what you dreamt about?"

"It was you. But, you tried to kill me with your power or something..."

"Power?" The man asked.

"Yeah..."

"Interesting" He said to himself, his features arranged in an intrigued manner.

"What's interesting?"

"Nothing, just thinking of something else." The man smiled at Devesh, but he felt a sinking feeling in the pit of his stomach, like the man was hiding something.

"What did you say your name was a-again?" Devesh asked, afraid his nightmare would end up truly happening.

"Oh, my name?" The man bared his teeth, in something that was definitely not a smile.

Devesh had an overwhelming sense of deja vu, as if he had just witnessed this happen. Suddenly, the scene he viewed in his dream came back to him.

Devesh watched as his nightmare slowly became real, and the man's smile elongated once again, his eyes turning as red as an Ironan's blood.

Devesh woke up, and this time he wasn't in his school infirmary. He prayed, hoping this was not another freaky dream. Sadly, his prayers were left unanswered. Though he was awake, his consciousness involuntarily slipped back into his shaky state of sleep, followed by his constant nightmarish visions.

Visions A voice seemed to say in his head *Is that what these are?*

No. The other replied. *They are reality. This is what it will be like from now on.*

Devesh felt like an outsider in his own thoughts, detached from what these voices seemed to be saying.

As soon as he heard the last voice's statement, he ended up believing it himself. He felt so powerless, hopeless, that he had no choice but to agree and continue undergoing the nightmares.

This time, he did not see his school's infirmary, but, instead, he woke up in a collapsing white chamber. He tried to move his feet, but as he looked down, he realised they were gone. His legs ended in wisps of trailing white fog.

His figure was translucent and made of the unsettling pale smoke. Devesh drifted around with a body that was no body at all.

Am I a ghost now? His mind seemed to wonder. *Am I dead? Did that man kill me?*

These unanswered questions seemed to swirl in his head as he watched the scene unfold before him.

He was able to recognise Ayan carrying an unconscious Alera through the crumbling white ruins. Soon, seemingly out of nowhere, he dropped down as well, his body unmoving

Asaya and a woman who resembled her were right at their heels. Asaya fell too, hit by an unseen danger.

Devesh's manner was unusually detached, as if he was the audience of the movie that was their disastrous lives.

He watched as the woman, possibly their mother, reached inch by inch towards her shoe.

Slowly, he grew intrigued, wondering if this was truly what was happening. He noticed a flit of movement between them, occasionally running about, too fast to be seen by the human eye.

Slowly but surely, the woman made her way towards whatever she was hiding in her boots. Her boots were sturdy, and lined with fur.

They look like ugg boots made for hunting... Devesh noted.

In one swift movement, she grabbed a pistol gun from her boot.

That's ridiculous. Whatever they're going against is way too fast for a gun-

Devesh never finished the thought, because he realised that he seemed to have drastically underestimated the capabilities of these species.

Her aim was near-perfect, hitting the unseen runner square in the forehead.

She bent towards her children's unconscious bodies, unsure how to wake them up.

Devesh had a feeling, something seemed to be pulling him towards their unmoving forms.

He ran a hand through Ayan's head, whispering 'wake up' into his mind.

Ayan woke up with a jolt, "Who said that?"

"Said what?" asked his mother, her eyebrows crinkling.

Ayan pales. "Nothing."

Devesh hears his unsaid words, *If she didn't hear it, I shouldn't worry her…*

Am I reading his mind? Devesh starts to wonder. *Is this even real?*

His mind dazed, he repeats the same action to Asaya and Alera, watching them search for his invisible form with wide, scared eyes.

What is happening to me?

Chapter 38
The Reunion

Present day,

Refugee Organisation of the Universe, Moon No. 97 of Planet Evian, Magellanic Cloud.

"What should we do now?" asked Ayan, still shook by his unusual wake-up call.

"Search for the others, obviously!" snapped Asaya, annoyed at the fact that she was unconscious, hence unable to help.

Alera sighed, "Fine, let's go."

Aya, though grateful, was still wondering about how they woke up so suddenly, claiming to hear a voice in their heads.

They made their way to the left, after yet another argument regarding what direction is more safe.

Aya trailed behind, seemingly unaware of where they were going.

They continued making their way through the littered clearing, most of them still dazed by the previous events. The group finally reached another crumbling cell, and began to search for their friends' familiar faces.

"You guys finally found us!" A voice cried from behind them.

Ayan's head swivelled in the direction of the voice, Alera, Aya and Asaya following suit, expecting to see either Priya's or Aakriti's hopeful face.

And, that was exactly what they witnessed.

Chapter 39
THE DEFEAT OF THE UNDEFEATABLE

Present day,

Refugee Organisation of the Universe, Moon No. 97 of Planet Evian, Magellanic Cloud.

Figuring out what the dragon's weakness was, was honestly the easy part for Azul.

Taking advantage of that vulnerability to defeat the serpent, now that was the hard part.

Azul began to continue his conversation with the creature, trying his best to seem as if he was not stalling.

He realised that if he got the dragon talking, soon it would be simple enough to trap it.

Yuvunans were quite a cunning species, but they often believed themselves to be above the rest of us, which meant they underestimated everyone's abilities.

And, of course, they were unduly egoistic.

Using these qualities to defeat them is difficult indeed, but Yununans were extremely skilled at combat, fighting with the creature would essentially mean his death wish.

So, now, Azul had no choice but to somehow, some way, make this creature walk right into his trap.

"Say, what's your name?" Azul asked. "I can't just call you 'dragon', can I?"

The creature let out one of its horrible cackles. "I'm not just a dragon, you see, unlike most Yuvunans, I have the ability to transform into all the species in the Universe, not just one."

Azul finally found his opening.

"Oh really?" He forced a tone of fascination into his voice. "Even the tiniest of creatures?"

"Why, yes, of course."

"Well, since I have no hope of rescue or escape… would you please entertain me?" Azul said, acting as if hopeless and bored. "I could use a bit of fun in my last moments, don't you think?"

"Yes, yes, sure, puny man."

"Really? Then can you turn into a small rat?"

The dragon let out another cackle. "Do you really think I'm that stupid?"

Azul smiled wide. "No. Of course not."

Before he knew it, the serpent creature tumbled to the ground, tripping over the thread that Azul oh-so-carefully wound around its feet. He pried the thread from his sturdy thick coat when the Yuvunan was preoccupied bragging about his abilities.

Azul immediately detached the stun-gun from his leg and shot the dragon until his body went limp, his face frozen mid-scream.

"Now, how the heck do we get out of this place?"

Chapter 40
THE FINAL ESCAPE

Present day,

Refugee Organisation of the Universe, Moon No. 97 of Planet Evian, Magellanic Cloud.

"Priya! Aakriti!" A voice seemed to say.

Everyone was too overcome with relief to be able to realise who voiced the thought that crossed all of their minds. "You're alive!"

They both seemed quite bruised, their clothes in tatters and skin coated with layers of dust and grime.

"A bit battered, but alive nonetheless." Asaya continued, a smile spreading across her face.

Suddenly, the sound of a huge thud seemed to echo around the clearing.

"What was that?" Ayan asked, his relief slowly dissipating into panic.

It was too easy, way too easy…

Unbeknown to him, the people around him shared the same thought.

A ping sounded from everyone's boots.

"What was *that*?" asked Aakriti.

Azul's voice sounded from below. "An emergency communications device, what humans commonly refer to as a 'walkie-talkie.' Its attached to your boots, pick it up"

"Alright, your Ironans are way cooler than you seem." Priya said. "Gotta truly give you guys credit sometimes"

"Listen to me carefully." Azul commanded through the walkie-talkie. "I managed to momentarily render the dragon unconscious. So, now, you all must follow my instructions for an escape route I discovered by studying the map on the screens."

"First, turn right..."

Azul began to describe the route out of the compound, and no one uttered a word, too astonished by their luck at being able to finally leave this prison.

"It really worked out, didn't it?" Alera whispered as Azul told them to move towards the left.

As they turned left, they entered another prison cell, where they encountered ...no one.

"Phew." Ayan said in response. "I thought this was going to be a 'you spoke too soon' moment."

"Thank the Lord of Astra it's not. Keep it moving." Azul's voice echoed. "Turn towards the right-most corridor..."

He resumed his directions one again.

"And, to your left right now should be multiple one-man spacecrafts." He finished. "Each of you enter one and leave the planet."

They began to count the spaceships.

There were only six.

"Azul, what about you?" asked Aya.

They heard Azul sigh. "Me? Don't worry about me. I'll find some way out with the rest of the prisoners. You all must escape safely."

"What do you mean?" Aakriti raged. "I'm not leaving the planet without you!"

They could almost hear the bittersweet smile in Azul's commanding tone. "I'm afraid you don't have a choice."

"What do you mean, 'I don't have a choice'?" Aakriti burst out.

"If all of you want to make it out of here alive, you must take your respective spaceships and leave." Azul said.

"Otherwise, there is a high chance we all remained trapped here forever, because the stun-gun I used on the dragon isn't going to keep him down for much longer.

"But, how will you deal with him?" questioned Ayan.

"I have my ways. I'm much more experienced than you believe, Ayan." replied Azul. "But, if I have to keep all of you safe and alive, it will be much harder, and to ensure all of your survival, I must ask you to leave this moon."

"You're going to come back, right?" Aakriti asked, her voice laced with undertones of worry and fear.

"Yes, of course."said Azul in response, his intonation forcibly hopeful.

Everyone realised that he himself was not sure of his safe return, and appreciated his sacrifice in their hearts.

Tears began to race down Aakriti's cheeks and the others followed suit, their eyes growing damp and sniffles tickling their noses.

"You'll make it alive, Azul." A voice said again.

Their shared thoughts and emotions represented their unity as a team. Without a member, it would feel empty, hopeless, even, so they all prayed for Azul's escape and safe return to Astra.

In a remote moon, revolving around an uninhabited planet in an unknown galaxy, I doubt any god truly heard their prayers.

Epilogue

The Way Back Home

Preview of The Chasm, Part 2

The rest of the crew strapped themselves into their respective spaceships with a sombre mood.

Each of the spacecrafts took off, emitting successive 'whoosh' noises.

"Should we set the course for Earth or Astra?" inquired Ayan through the walkie-talkie.

"Astra. We need to send Aakriti and Priya back to Earth, along with the other boy." replied Asaya.

"Other boy?" Priya questioned. "What 'other boy'?"

"Oh no, oh no, please don't tell me-" Aakriti was cut off by Alera,

"Yes, Devesh somehow got to Astra."

Aakriti replied, "As if we didn't have enough worries already."

"Truly, children, I believe we should maintain the solemn mood for Azul's sake, at least?" Aya pitched in.

"Mother, we'll be arriving soon enough to rescue him anyways." retorted Ayan.

"What?" Aya said, worry creeping into her voice. "Of course not! Some trusted adults, including me, will be leading the mission for Azul's rescue. Not you lot!"

"We have enough experience in inter-galactic rescue missions after this event," said Asaya.

"No you don't!"

The argument was unduly prolonged and their conversation continued millions of light years back to Astra, back to home.

www.ingramcontent.com/pod-product-compliance
Lightning Source LLC
LaVergne TN
LVHW041214150826
845673LV00001B/399

* 9 7 9 8 8 9 5 5 6 3 8 3 0 *